*Seven
Was the Padre's Number*

BOOKS BY HENRY JAMES

Seven Was the Padre's Number
The Curse of the San Andres

Seven Was the Padre's Number

A Novel by
Henry James

Exposition Press   New York

FIRST EDITION

© 1973 by Henry James

All rights reserved, including the right of reproduction in whole or in part, in any form or by any means, electronic or mechanical, including photocopying, recording, or by any information storage and retrieval system, without permission in writing from the Publisher. Inquiries should be addressed to Exposition Press, Inc., 50 Jericho Turnpike, Jericho, N.Y. 11753

ISBN 0-682-47784-2

Manufactured in the United States of America
Published simultaneously in Canada by Transcanada Books

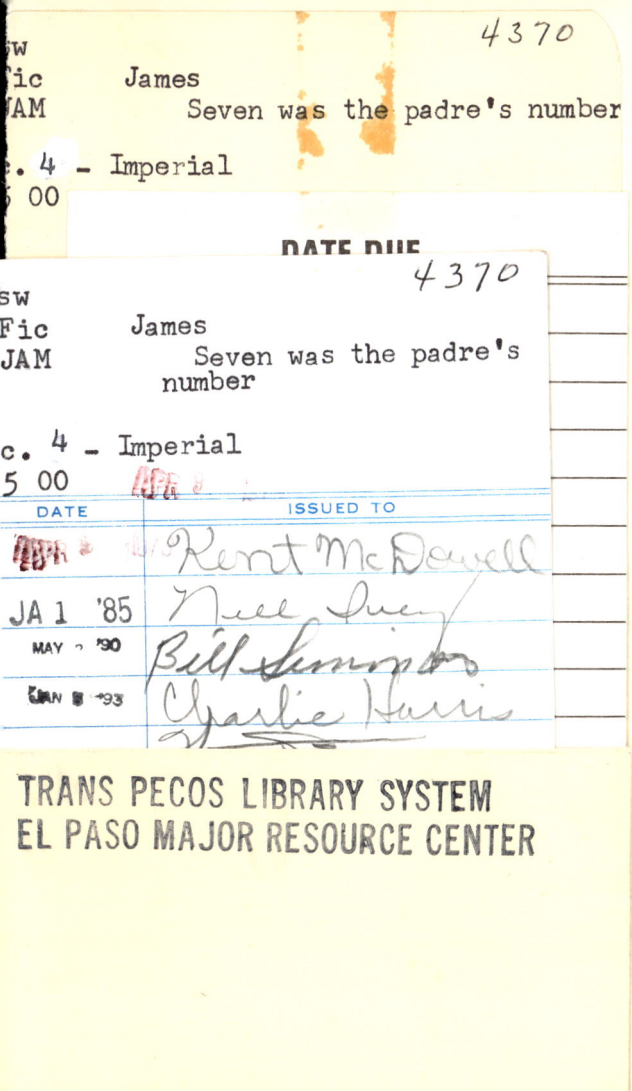

```
sw
Fic     James
JAM         Seven was the padre's number

c. 4 - Imperial
5 00
```

```
sw
Fic     James
JAM         Seven was the padre's
            number

c. 4 - Imperial
5 00
```

4370

TRANS PECOS LIBRARY SYSTEM
EL PASO MAJOR RESOURCE CENTER

This book is dedicated
to
All treasure hunters

Espero que halle el tesoro que busca.
I hope you find the treasure you seek.

Contents

Preface	9
Seven Is the Holy Number	10
Map Showing Route of the Padre and Colony	12
Prologue	13
Seven Was the Padre's Number	21
Epilogue	157

Preface

Lost mines and treasures have been legends in the Southwest since Coronado's search for gold in 1540. It is said that every legend has its basis in fact, but few have ever been found.

This novel tells of a dying Spanish soldier, who made his deathbed confession, to a padre, of deserting the King's Army to work a rich find of gold ore, far to the north.

Drought had plagued the land and the people of the hacienda were facing starvation. The appearance of the soldier and his story of a rich deposit of gold seemed a good omen. After much persuasion, the padre agreed to lead his people north to a new life, abandoning the Church and the hacienda.

The long and perilous journey, across waterless deserts, plagued by hostile Indians, seemed impossible at times but, finally, their destination was reached and the soldier's words proved true. Happiness prevailed among the people as they lived and worked in the quiet valley. Then disaster struck, when Spanish dragoons apeared on the scene.

Over a century and a half passed before the events of the story came to light. An American "gringo" stumbled onto a cave with skeletons, documents, and a treasure worth millions in its depths. The treasure is believed to be that of Padre La Rue and his unfortunate colony.

Henry James

Seven Is the Holy Number

Seven is the holy number. There are seven days in the week, seven phases of the moon, every seventh year is Sabbatical, and seven times seven years was Jubilee. There are seven ages in the life of man, seven divisions in the Lord's Prayer, seven Bibles, seven churches of Asia, seven Graces, seven Deadly Sins, seven Senses, seven Sorrows of the Virgin, seven Virtues, seven Joys of the Virgin, seven Precious Things of the Buddhas, seven Sleepers of Ephesus, seven Lamps of Architecture. The Apostles chose seven deacons, Enoch, who was translated was seventh from Adam, Jesus Christ was the seventy-seventh in a direct line. Our Lord spoke seven times on the cross, on which He was seven hours. He appeared seven times and after seven times seven days He sent the Holy Ghost. There appeared seven golden candlesticks and the seven golden stars in the hand of him that was in the mind; seven lambs before the seven Spirits of God; the book with seven seals; the lamb with seven horns and seven eyes; seven Angels bearing seven plaques, and seven vials of wrath. The vision of Daniel was seventy weeks; and the elders of Israel were seventy. There were also seven heavens, seven planets, seven stars, seven wise men, seven Champions of Christendom, seven notes of music, seven primary colors, seven Sacraments of the Catholic Church, and seven wonders of the world. The seventh son is still endowed with pre-eminent wisdom; and the seventh son of a seventh son is still thought to possess the power of healing diseases spontaneously.

In seven languages, seven signs, and languages in seven foreign nations, look for the seven cities of gold. Seventy miles north of El Paso del Norte in the seventh peak Soledad, these cities have seven sealed doors, three sealed toward the rising of the Sol sun, three sealed toward the setting of the Sol sun, one deep within Casa del Cueva de Oro, high noon, and receive health, wealth, and honor.

> By the Holy Father La Rue
> 1802 A.D. Sealed to Father Rheuschone of Madrid, Spain.

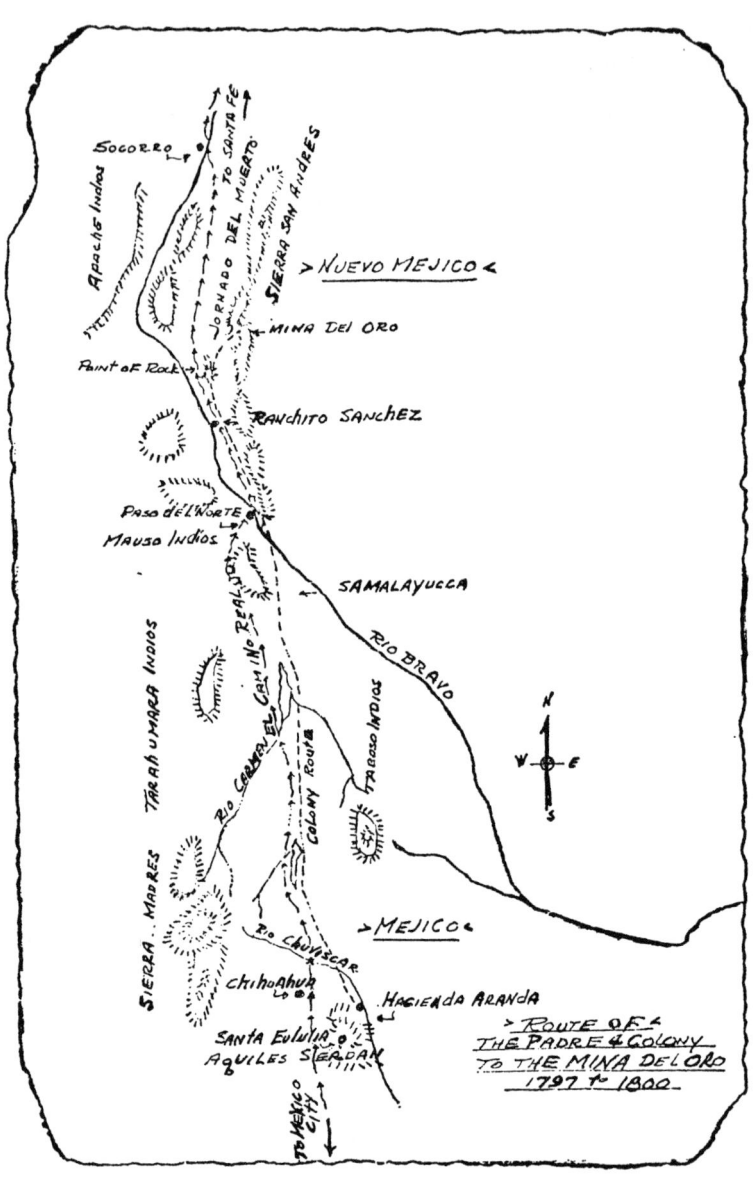

Prologue

The town of Socorro lies on the edge of the Rio Grande valley, where the river widens, spreading out to a mile or more, winding through bosques of cottonwoods and willows and bled by ditches that irrigate the fields. An old town, almost as old as the highway that cuts through the central plaza, once the lifeline between Santa Fe and Mexico City, El Camino Réal has been the main line of travel for over three hundred years.

On an afternoon in late May, the air carried the scent of plowed fields and the springing green of crops, bursting through the warm earth. Bees hummed among the late blossoms in the orchards. A boy of ten, kept after school to help the teacher, came out of the open door of the adobe schoolhouse, rubbing his hands on his overalls to remove the chalk dust. His dark curls were damp in the moist heat of late spring and little beads of sweat stood on his forehead.

His thoughts were far ahead of his impatient feet as he hurried down the lane. Soon school would be out for the summer and, this year, his father had promised that he could go with his grandfather to the mountains. Every year the sheep were driven to the high meadows to grow fat on the lush mountain grass. The old man stayed with them until the chill winds of fall signaled that it was time to bring them back down to the valley.

Happiness glowed in his eyes as he thought of a whole summer with his beloved grandfather. Nights were the best, he considered. Then, by the campfire, the old man would tell him stories of when, as a young man, he had fought fierce beasts and savage Apaches. Now, mostly coyotes got after the lambs and had to be driven off with clubs and stones.

His mind was full of these things when he saw Miguel, his best friend, running toward him from the plaza, waving a newspaper. Miguel sold papers, since the death of his father, to help his mother feed the three youngest of the family.

"Hey Tirso! Wait up! I want to show you!"

Tirso stopped and his friend shoved a paper toward him.

"*Mira!* A big story! A gringo found a cave in the mountains! Full of gold! There were bones, *también,* of some *póbres,* who died in the cave! Just like the story your grandfather tells. You think it is the same, no?"

Tirso took the paper, slowly spelling out the printed words. Then he looked up, excitement kindling in his face.

"It sounds the same," he said. "Let us show this to my father. He will know."

"*Ahé!*" Miguel shouted. "You think he will claim a share of the gold? You will be rich!" He was dancing up and down, unable to stand still.

"Ah, Miguel," Tirso scorned. "When does a gringo share with *mejicáños?* What he finds, he will keep. But I must tell my father, quickly."

"Wait, Tirso. That is my last paper. I must take the money to the paper office. Then I will go with you."

Tirso hesitated and Miguel went on, "Maybe my boss, Señor Pembroke, will print a story about your grandfather."

Tirso frowned. "My father will be angry if I do not hurry and, anyway, I do not know if my grandfather would like to be in the paper."

"Ah come on," Miguel pleaded. "It will take only *un minúto* and then we will go to your home. You know, I was the one to show you the story in the paper."

Persuaded, Tirso followed his friend across the plaza to a small, weatherbeaten building of once-white clapboards. A newly painted sign over the door proclaimed, Socorro Bugle. John Pembroke, editor. Edging into the door way behind Miguel, Tirso saw Mr. Pembroke, who was not only editor but printer and reporter of the weekly paper, bent over setting type.

Miguel dug his hand into his pocket and piled some small coins on the table.

"I have sold all the papers, señor. Do you wish me to take more?"

"They are all gone, boy," the man answered. "I am setting

up a second edition. That story about the gold sold 'em fast." He paused to scoop up the coins and, counting a few into Miguel's hand, thrust them into his pocket.

Miguel shuffled his feet and said, hesitantly, "Señor, this is my friend, Tirso Aguirre. His grandfather knows about this cave. He has told many times about it and of the poor people who died there."

"What did you say, boy?" Pembroke asked sharply, stopping his work. "How could his grandfather know about it when it was just discovered?"

A new voice broke in. "You are a newcomer, Señor Pembroke, and have not heard the stories my people tell." The speaker was a tall man, weighing perhaps two hundred pounds.

"Mayor Rodriguez!" exclaimed Pembroke. "You mean there is such a story?"

"Oh yes. Señor Aguirre has been telling it for years and his father before him."

"I must talk to him then. It will make a good follow-up story for the second and maybe a third edition." As he spoke he was already pulling off his green eye-shade and apron, hanging them on a nail.

"Where can I find your grandfather, boy, what's-your-name, Tirso?"

"He lives out on the Magdalena road, Señor. Maybe three miles. If you will come with me, I will ask my father if I can show you his house," Tirso answered, a little shy in the presence of the mayor.

Hastening out, they were stopped by a dark-robed figure that stepped in front of them.

"Ah, Señores," the priest said, calmly. "You are in great haste for such a warm afternoon."

The men snatched off their hats and bowed with reverence.

"Father Markos," the mayor said smiling. "You are just in time. My friend here, being new in town, has never heard Señor Aguirre's story of the colony from Chihuahua, who found a great treasure of gold in a cavern to the south and were murdered by dragoons. You have seen the paper?"

"Yes. I came to ask if any more was known about this strange discovery by an American?"

"Nothing, except what was printed, Father." Mr. Pembroke spoke respectfully. "Do you think there is any connection with the old tale?"

"There is similarity, if it is true," the priest nodded. "Who can tell if they are the same?"

"I wish to talk to Señor Aguirre," Pembroke said. "Since I am a stranger, perhaps you will all come with me. The man will no doubt talk more freely in the presence of the mayor and his priest." He bowed to each of them.

"I will be glad to join you, Señor," the priest answered. "I have been meaning to see the Aguirres on a little matter for the Church. Some painting that is sadly needed."

The editor led the way to an old Model A car. Its battered appearance showed acquaintance with many a rough road. There was a little difficulty in starting but the old engine coughed, sputtered, and backfired and, finally, took off with a jerk.

Tirso's father was startled by their descent and amazed by the news they brought, but he hastily squeezed into the back seat with the mayor and the boys, who were determined not to be left behind.

The grandfather was equally startled when they arrived in his yard and piled out of the car, all talking at once. Little Tirso ran to his side and seized his hand, anxious to be first with the news.

"Grandfather!" he exclaimed. "The cave of your grandfather has been found! A gringo discovered it and it is full of gold, just as you have told us. *Esquéletos, también,* skeletons of the *póbres viéjos* who died there."

The old man looked from one to the other in the group. His tall figure was as erect as a boy's, his curly grey hair was thick and his dark eyes were bright.

"Señores," he said. "You do me honor to come to my small home. Come in and seat yourselves. You wish to hear my story, which is the story of my grandfather." He turned to the boy who still clung tightly to his hand and said affectionately, "We will tell them, eh, boy? Perhaps now, they will believe the story of my grandfather, the *Priméro* Tirso, when he wandered out of the desert of the Jornado del Muerto with the girl, Dolores, who was my grandmother."

Seven
Was the Padre's Number

CHAPTER ONE

Shadows lengthened as the sun dropped slowly toward the crest of the blue sierras. To the boy, squatting among the boulders at the top of a limestone outcropping, keeping watch over the road below, it seemed as if the rays were reluctant to leave the parched yellow land. He reflected that this was the third year of the drought. The streams and waterholes were almost dry and the cattle suffered. The burned grass of the range held little nourishment. All summer, Don Tomás had cursed the lack of rain, and good Father La Rue had prayed faithfully in the little chapel on the hacienda, to no avail.

From his vantage point, Tirso could see in a wide circle across the broken country of northern Mexico. Far to the west, the blue wall of the Sierra Madres rose, their high peaks and deep shadowy canyons darkened as the sun lowered. Behind him spread the broad expanse of Don Tomás Adánda's hacienda. Ancient trees outlined the course of the Rio Chuviscar that marked the eastern boundary of his land, held under a King's grant for a hundred years. The buildings around the placita of the hacienda were concealed by the tree tops, but Tirso could see the bell tower of the little chapel and the barns and stables with a web of corrals spreading about them. Farther east, across the river, was Aquíles Serdán, the mountain where the Santa Eulalia mines poured forth a wealth of silver. North on the river, the buildings of the city of Chihuahua were barely discernible. Only the twin towers of the great cathedral could be identified above the huddle of the town that nestled in a crescent of the mountains.

The dark, alert eyes in the thin face of the boy turned back to the closed gates of the hacienda. No sign of the party of men that had ridden in to the *placita* that morning. He had been carrying water to fill the trough behind the house for his mother's cow and the goat, when the six men had appeared, all of them with muskets. The absence of pack animals told him they were not casual travelers or hunters. Bitter experience had taught him caution in the face of the unknown and, with a helpless glance at the cow, he had fastened a rope around the neck of the goat and slipped out into the brush. One of the many gullies that cut the hacienda covered his retreat until he reached the foot of the hill. Here he tied the goat in the brush and climbed up the rocky boulder-strewn slope to the top.

Through the afternoon hours he had crouched there, watching for the men to leave. Sweat trickled down from under his battered sombrero and he took it off and mopped his face. He cuffed the dust from the stained leather, pridefully. Not every *muchácho* had a real sombrero This one had become his as a mark of the *Patrón's* favor. Although it was well worn when he had received it, it was a hat of distinction compared to the straw *petátes* of the others. Someday, he promised himself, he would have things of his own. Things such as Don Tomás wore. Buckskins and a horse to ride, maybe a big black with silver on his saddle. Perhaps a silver hatband also.

Already he was twelve. Tibúrcio, the *mayor-dómo,* had permitted him to ride on the *córrida* this year with the *vaquéros.* If it had not been for the sickness which kept his mother in her bed, moaning and tossing with fever, he might have gone with them to drive the steers to market. Tirso sighed, thinking how fine they had looked, with Don Tomás and Tibúrcio in front and the *vaquéros,* dashing their mounts this way and that, shouting and whacking the fat beef rumps to keep the herd moving. He sighed again. It would have been wonderful to ride with the herd to Chihuahua. He was reminded of the fiesta of San Juan last June, when he had gone with the others from the haciénda to Chihuahua. Crowds from the whole countryside mingled in delighted merrymaking with travelers from both north and south, who moved along the great *Camino Réal* that joined Santa Fe and Mexico City.

That was one of the good memories. The sounds and smells of the carnival, the fascination of the caravans and the riders from the north. Someday, he would take the highway and ride north to the Rio Bravo and, perhaps beyond. I would ride and ride forever and never stop, he thought, resting his chin on his hand, picturing the north country the men had talked about around the fires.

A wind from the west was coming up. Streamers of sand lifted along the road and rose, twisting into tawny spirals that marched along the plain, finally breaking and vanishing. The cool air stirred the damp curls that hung about his face and brought him back from his dreams of the far country. His eyes went to the gates, still closed, with no sign of the party.

A frown wrinkled his forehead as the thought of his mother came to his mind. The mysterious fever had held for days. None of the women would come near her. Only the good Father La Rue came daily to pray and to put cloths wet with cool water on her face. I am all that she has, he thought. I cannot leave her alone. For six years they had lived alone, since the day when Tibúrcio had brought his father home, a limp burden, lying across his saddle. He remembered his mother's despairing scream and the tightening of his throat as he saw the blurred patch of blood on his father's shirt, darkening as it dried.

"Apaches," Tibúrcio had told them. A small band had come racing down on the men in a hollow of the hills, while they were doctoring a wormy calf. For some reason known to themselves, the Indians had paused only long enough to loose a few arrows, most of which fell short, and then raced on. One arrow had found a mark. When the others had recovered from the surprise of the attack, they had found his father, Tirso the elder, dying and brought him home. Tirso would not soon forget his mother's sobbing night after night or the emptiness that still filled him at the thought of that gray evening.

A scrambling sound behind him turned him quickly. Tense, he watched the slope, then relaxed as a familiar mop of red hair appeared.

"Lucíta!" he exclaimed. "What are you doing here? Why do you follow me? Is anything wrong?"

The girl plumped herself down beside him, panting from the climb.

"Let me catch my breath." Her dark eyes sparkled under curling lashes. She rubbed a long scratch on her arm. "See what the thorns did to me. And I have torn my skirt too. My mother will be furious." She smiled at him. "But I do not care. I saw you leave and I would have followed then but my mother caught me and made me help her twist chili for drying. *Pués,* how my hands sting." She rubbed them in the dirt. "When she went to start the fire for supper, I slipped away. I knew where you would be. Staring into the sky and dreaming of your beloved north country."

Tirso turned back to watch the road and the gates. "You rattle like an empty cart, Lucíta. What did those men want? They have been here for hours."

"They came to collect more taxes. They suspected that some things might have been hidden from them when they were here before." Her eyes snapped. "So the *cabrónes* came back to see if there was more." Her lip curled.

Tirso whirled to face her. "More! Ah, they are thieves! They wish to leave us nothing! They took the largest portion when they were here before. How Don Tomás cursed after they had left." He grinned at the thought. "That is a man who expresses himself well. But what is taking these *ladrónes* so long? It is three hours, by the sun, since they came.'

"Can you not guess, *Chíco?*" Lucíta said, contemptuously, wrapping her arms around her knees. "They are, of course, in the *cása* of the *patrón,* swilling his wine and brandy like pigs."

"No wonder Don Tomás curses," Tirso said, thoughtfully. "This is the third year of the drought. The cattle do not flourish and the crops were hardly worth gathering. Of the little we have, the tax collectors take what they want and leave us with almost empty storehouses. God must be angry with the poor people."

Movement near the gates of the hacienda caught his eye.

"Quiet, Lucíta! They come! At last."

He watched intently as the party of men emerged onto the road. A cart followed them now and they were driving some stock. He could not see clearly for the dust that boiled up about them. Lucíta rose to peer over the rocks and he seized her hand and pulled her down.

Seven Was the Padre's Number

"Be quiet, girl," he commanded. "Do you want them to find us? And perhaps take you with them? That red hair of your shines like a fire, in the sun."

As the riders came nearer, Tirso distinguished some mules, three cows, and a number of goats. Two men rode in front, in buckskin pants and jackets and low-crowned black sombreros. Across their high-peaked Spanish saddles, muskets glinted in the sun. Four others pushed the animals along in a veil of dust. The cart followed at a little distance, driven by Pablo from the hacienda. It was rounded high with confiscated goods, with a wagon sheet lashed over the load. As the party passed beneath, Tirso leaned out and saw his mother's cow among the stock. Anger reddened his face and he beat at the rocks with his clenched fists.

"The cow was all we had," his voice was choked. "Why were they allowed to seize her? What can the King need of our one cow? For him a few *pesos*, but to my mother, she meant life."

Lucíta's dark eyes were warm with sympathy. She put her arms around him and pressed a kiss on his cheek. "It is too bad, Tirso. But what can you do? You know what happens to any who defy the King's men."

"*Sí*, I know," the boy answered. "They can shoot me or they can take me away to work in the mines. Then my mother would have no one."

"I am sorry, Tirso, but that is the way it is. We cannot do otherwise than obey." Their eyes followed the receding party.

"It will not always be so," Tirso said darkly. "I am twelve and already I have proved that I can do the work of a man. Someday Don Tomás will look at me and say, 'Tirso Aguirre, you are as good a man as your father, who was the best *vaquéro* I ever had.' I will be big and powerful like him and I will ride north to the new country on the Rio Bravo. It will be different then. I will not have to hide behind rocks. I will go where I will and men will take off their hats when I ride by." He held his head high and lifted his sombrero in salute to the image he had created.

Lucíta tightened her arms about him. "Tirso, why must you go north? It is all you ever talk about. What is so wonderful in this wild, faraway country?"

"I do not know, Lucíta, but when I think of it, something inside me sings. When we went to the fiesta in Chihuahua, on San Juan's Day, I listened to the men who came with the caravans from the new province. They talked of the good land along the great river and of the mountains with tall trees. Do you know they pay money to meat hunters? And trappers get many *pésos* for furs. A man can be rich."

"I heard stories too. About the wild animals and the Indians. Great cats that leap on you and huge yellow bears, bigger than a horse. You could be killed."

"There is that possibility," Tirso admitted.

"Or scalped, like old Pablo who lives alone because no woman can bear to live with his horrible face. Ugh! All sagging and twisted even though the Father did his best. It would have been better if the Indians had killed him."

"My father was murdered by Apaches. It was not better. It was great sadness of loss and much hardship for my mother and me."

"*Sí*, that is true. Perhaps if one is loved, it would not matter how horrible the appearance," Lucíta considered. "For a man anyway. A woman would rather die than be disfigured." She pulled a curling red lock through her fingers. "Men are lucky. A girl can only stay at home and twist chile and cook and wash clothes. What fun is there in that? I would give much to go with you. To ride like a man and race ahead of all the others. It would be like flying and I would be free, not chained to a wash tub."

Tirso chuckled and then laughed. Lucíta looked at him defensively.

"What amuses you? Do you think you are the only one who loves freedom?"

"No, my wild one." Tirso answered, still laughing. "I was thinking of your mother's face if she could hear you. Ho! She would explode."

Lucíta sprang up, stamping her feet. "Who cares, *muchácho!* When the right time comes, I will go! You will see." Red flags burned in her cheeks, as she left him.

Tirso looked after her in amazement, wondering what he had said to make her angry. Then he rose and followed, stopping to untie the goat. Pulling the little animal after him, he hurried home. As his thin brown legs flashed through the dust, his problems returned to depress him. Questions crowded his mind. To get the answers he must find the Father.

The collectors of the King moved in a compact group. The leader, Captain Barrerras, was anxious to make Chihuahua before darkness closed on them. This was Apache country, and the hours of twilight were the favorite time of the savages for attack. Barrerras' eyes swept the broad plain and the rolling hills, watchful for any sign of movement. Maco, the big chief of the Apaches, sent his bands to strike, deadly as rattlesnakes, sometimes within sight of the forts.

The men rode silent, red-eyed, and thin tempered. Alkali powdered their clothing and rimmed their mouths whitely. Barrerras' lieutenant, a young man, slender in his black leather jacket, appeared nervous. He glanced around at the desolate, hot country with dissatisfaction. Hawking the dust from his throat, he spoke to the captain.

"Capitán Barrerras, this return visit to the Aránda haciénda was an idea of merit. It was plain that much of the taxable goods had been concealed from us."

"*Sí.*" Barrerras answered shortly, his eyes on a plume of dust ahead. "I know these people and their sly tricks. This is your first journey to serve the viceroy as a collector. You will learn."

The lieutenant pulled a *panuélo* from his jacket and wiped the sweat and dust from his face. "Angels of Christ, but it is hot," he groaned. "The dishonesty of these peons, making ruses such as this expedition necessary! They should be punished severely. In the south of Mexico, we simply shoot them. Thus we not only punish the guilty, but give a warning to others."

Captain Barrerras was still watching the cone of dust. He

decided that it was no more than three riders, apparently from the village.

"Well, we do not shoot them here," he said. "They are needed to work the great mines of Santa Eulalia. The small amount of taxes to be squeezed out of them is inconsiderable beside the stream of silver that flows from the mines. I do not think the powers of government would be happy if there was a reduction in the cargoes of the plate ships. The King might ask unanswerable questions if the usual shipments of his favorite metals did not arrive."

The lieutenant glanced quickly at the captain and a trace of impatience crept into his voice. "Nonetheless, these dogs are familiar with the tax system. For more than two hundred years, since Cortez marched into Mexico City, there have been taxes. How else would it have been possible to build a country out of these disorganized, ignorant *Indios,* who must be dug out of the brush where they hide like animals?"

"These *Indios* may be ignorant but they can strike savagely." The captain fingered a long scar that streaked his brown face whitely. "It is unwise to push them too far. My grandfather remembers the hunger riots in Mexico City, when the starving natives swept through the streets like animals, burning and killing.

"Revolt! Impossible!" the lieutenant gave a bark of laughter. "They have no arms, no ammunition, and no leader. The beggars are concerned only with getting enough food for their empty bellies."

"Nothing in this life is impossible," said the captain, shrugging his shoulders in contemptuous tolerance of his companion's youth and inexperience. "There are rumors of a priest in the south who is talking too much to the peons about their rights."

"You mean the Franciscan, Hidalgo? That will never come to anything. He will not dare to rise against the armies of the King."

The captain laughed, in his turn. "Who knows what goes on in a country of this size, my friend. A breeze of today is suddenly a tornado tomorrow. Do not underestimate the priests."

Seven Was the Padre's Number

Reining his horse around, he spurred back along the line of animals. "*Ándale! Ándale!* For the love of God, are we to spend the night in this desolation? With the Apaches, perhaps?"

"No, *Señor*. I think Chihuahua is better. Plenty *mescál* and pretty women. Ah-hé!" One of the men answered. The others laughed.

"*Vámanos, hómbres!* Let us have a little speed. An hour will see us in Chihuahua. With the animals in the corral with the others, ready for the auction tomorrow, there will be nothing more required of you tonight."

His words had the necessary effect and the pace of the party increased.

Haciénda Aránda was quiet under the lowering sun. A quiet of bitterness and resentment. Father La Rue, emerging from the little chapel, felt and understood the animosity that gripped the people. He stood for a little, watching the delicate colors painting the western sky, presaging the fires of sunset. A tall, thin man, his long face was gaunt above the brown robe of the Franciscans. Deep-socketed black eyes surveyed the clustered houses. The evening breeze carried the pungent smell of wood smoke from the supper fires. Candle light glowed softly from the windows and the sounds of children playing came to his ears.

As he turned toward his small home nearby, a call halted him. Turning, he recognized the slight figure of Tirso, running toward the placita, jerking the goat along behind him. The boy slid down the crumbling bank of an arroya and scrambled up the other side, calling, "Father! Father! Wait for me!"

"Tirso, my young friend," the priest said sharply, noting the distress in the boy's face. "What is wrong?"

The boy came to him and dropped to his knees, whipping off his cherished sombrero. "Father, *que páso?* Those men, did you know they have driven off my mother's cow? I saw them. What will *mi mádre* do now? She cannot eat the *frijóles* and *tortíllas*. I gave her hot milk and sometimes even that would not stay down. What will I give her now?"

The priest's hand caressed the boy's head. "Captain Barrerras is a ruthless man. There is nothing to be gained by defying him, although I said all I could. If Don Aránda had been here. . . ." He paused and shrugged his shoulders. "But there is no doubt that they waited until the *patron* was well on his way before returning."

The boy's eyes sparkled with anger. "Those men are no better than murderers, Father. Ai-ee. Perhaps we are all better dead, where there is no hunger or thirst."

"Silence, boy!" the priest was stern. "God decides the matters of life and death." Then his voice softened and he patted the boy's head. "You need more prayer, *muchacho*, to drive anger from your heart. Go now, to your mother. Milk is not good for fever. I have a chicken stewing. Perhaps the broth will strengthen her. I will bring some, but first I must see to *el viéjo*, the old one, who was brought in from the desert. He is very sick."

The boy rose to his feet and stood, turning his hat in his hand, "He is one of them, is he not, Father? *Un soldádo?*" His tone was bitter.

"He is a soldier, yes," the priest answered. "I know little more than that. Since the men found him unconscious on the sand, he has had only a few lucid minutes. I fear the sun has done its work. Run along, boy, I will not be long."

He stood for a moment, looking after the slight figure with the despondent droop of the shoulders as Tirso moved across the beaten yellow clay of the placita and shook his head sadly. Then he turned toward the doorway of his home, his thoughts going to the dying man within.

CHAPTER TWO

The door stood wide and the padre stepped inside, grateful for the cool dimness inside the thick mud walls that defied the scorching sun. On a pallet near the door lay a man, his features so sharp with emaciation that it seemed the bones would break through the dry yellow skin. A mop of dirty white hair framed the thin face on the blanket. Beside him sat a young girl, bathing his face with a cloth which she dipped in a basin of cool water.

As the priest entered, the girl rose to her feet with a swift, graceful motion.

"Father, I think *el hómbre* is better. Twice he has opened his eyes. It is good, no?"

At the sound of her voice, the man's eyes opened again and fastened on the kindly face of the priest. Wide and dark, they probed his features anxiously, then, as he recognized the robe of the Franciscan, relief flooded them.

"*Dónde 'stóy?*" It was the barest whisper.

"You are at the hacienda of Don Tomás Aránda, my friend." The priest took his hand. "Near to *el cíudad de Chihúahua*."

Fear rose in the sick man's eyes. "Padre . . . Padre, you will not betray me?" He clutched the priest's hand. "Hide me, or I am a dead man."

The father was puzzled. He touched the man's forehead and found it cool and dry. The fever that had ridden him was gone and his mind was clear. He turned to the girl. "*Por favór*, Dolores, bring me a little wine for our patient. It will give him strength."

The girl glided away and the priest turned back to the sick man.

"Rest, *hómbre*. You are among friends. I do not know from whence you came or where you go. I will not ask. I am a servant of God and as such, my duty is to help my fellow man, not to judge him."

The man's intent gaze relaxed a little. "I trust you, Padre."

Dolores came with a flask and the priest took it and held it to the man's lips. He swallowed once, twice, eagerly and the priest withdrew the flask.

"Enough, for now, *mi amigo*. Later, you can have some broth."

He started to rise but the man's fingers grasped his robe. The weak voice was a little stronger.

"*Pádre*," he hesitated, "I was . . . I am a soldier in the

King's Army." The priest nodded. This much he had guessed. "I have been a bad one, Father. I deserted my company. If they find me, you will have saved my life for my executioners."

"You have sinned. I will pray for you until you are strong enough to pray for your own forgiveness. But now, rest. Have no fear. No one will look for you on this isolated hacienda, in the poor house of a priest."

The man's eyes held his for a moment, the muscles of his forehead knotted. Then he relaxed, satisfied, and his eyelids drooped. The father beckoned to the girl and stepped outside. She came quickly to his side, looking up at him questioningly.

"Dolores, my child, forget what you have heard. I should have sent you away. The less you know the better."

"Yes, Father." The answer was obedient. Her sweet face was lifted to him and her dark eyes were sad under the black wings of her hair parted and brushed smoothly back in a silky knot. "I am very sorry for him. Will he live?"

The priest shook his head, dubiously. "With the help of God, perhaps. I think not. He must have lain long in the sun before Pablo and Juanito found him." He was silent for a moment, thinking. At last he roused himself with a shrug of his broad shoulders. "Bring me a bowl of the broth of the chicken, Dolores. I am off to see how Tirso's mother is doing. Poor woman, the fever is burning her away to ashes."

It was late when the orange moon of August rose over the limestone cliffs of the Chihuahua mountains. Its rays lit the *placita* and glowed on the little white-walled church. In the deep shadow of the doorway, Father La Rue's robe stirred in the breeze of evening. He had sat, looking into the night, long after closing the eyes and folding the wasted hand of Magdalena Aguirre, long after he had murmured prayers for her soul. Magdalena had finished her life.

The wailing of the women, as they dressed and wrapped the body for the grave, filled the night. Outside the hut, the men squatted, chanting as was the custom. Tirso's desperate sobbing had quieted after Dolores led him back to the priest's house and soothed him to sleep.

The father's face was somber and his heart very heavy. Magdalena's husky voice, as she clutched her son's hand, beat in his mind. "There is no more for me, my son, but for you, there must be something better. Follow your dream and go to the north. There is nothing for you here. Go far and go fast, my son." Then her eyes had dulled and the flush of fever had greyed into the pallor of death.

"Is this all I can do for my people?" the priest asked himself. "Pray for their souls, marry them, christen their babies, give them absolution, and close their eyes?" He struck his knee with one fist. "It would take so little to make their lives bearable. Yet my letters to the Church go unanswered. I have told them of the drought, year after year. Surely they can spare a little from their coffers." Staring into the dark, he searched for an answer to come to him.

As the rays of moonlight probed into the shadowed doorway and crept upward lighting his face with the glow, his dark mood lifted. After all, he had accomplished much here on the Aránda estate. The years of drought had been hard but the people found comfort in the church. Time meant nothing out here. God willing, things would change for the better. If not this year, then next year. It required faith and prayer. Much prayer.

Rising, he turned slowly into his small house. Passing through the doorway, he saw the soldier was awake on his pallet. Beyond, on the priest's narrow bunk, the boy slept, face down. Beside him, Dolores sat on the floor, her eyes closed and her head pillowed on the edge of the cot.

Spreading a blanket beside the sick man, the father lay down, his eyes on the magic of the moonlight that flooded the world outside. Memories of other nights came to his mind. Moonlight on the splashing fountains and perfumed gardens of Castile, in Spain, where he had learned his rudiments from the Franciscan Fathers. Moonlight on the high seas, as he traveled to New Spain, full of hope and the impatient fire of youth. He sighed and the sick man turned his head questioningly. Answering the look, the priest spoke softly, not to disturb the others.

"What fools men are, *amigo*. What we desire greatly, we convince ourselves to be truth and, therefore, right."

The sick man considered the words and then nodded. "I too have discovered this to be true, Padre. Contentment is the only thing worth striving for and a man needs very little to be *conténto*."

"You are wise, *hómbre*." The priest agreed. "When I came to this country, I was very young and full of a vision of adventure in a wild new country. Ah, the dreams of gold and treasure that fired my brain."

"You are fortunate, Padre. You have peace. The gold of this country is cursed. It has brought me nothing but ill fortune. Look well at me. Antonio de Baca Rivera, sergeant-at-arms in His Majesty's army. Honored for bravery and devotion to duty. Yet you see before you *un hómbre ruíno,* forced to hide my face from all men. This tragedy was accomplished by gold."

The father made a clucking sound of sympathy. There was a little silence and then Rivera spoke again, his voice hardly more than a husky whisper.

"We were enroute to Santa Fe. The company was encamped near Point of Rocks on El Camino Reál. Three of us rode out to hunt. Meat for the camp you understand. The other two rode far ahead. I followed a deer trail down to a spring in the bottom of a bowl-shaped valley. In a little draw, I came upon a cave. It led back into the bowels of the mountain. Curiosity laid upon me and dismounting, I fashioned a torch and explored its depths. It was like a series of great rooms, Father, each larger than the preceding one. As I went on, I heard a murmur that grew louder and louder. Then I came into a huge cavern, larger than anything I had ever seen. The murmur had become a roar and I saw the source. A great underground river rushed across the floor of the cavern. It slid out from under the rock wall of one side and disapeared into the opposite wall. I stared into the sinister black water rushing from nowhere, until I was dizzy. At last, I forced my eyes away and looked about me at sheer walls of rock, rising high above. A glimmer of white caught my eye and my torch showed me a vein of white rock, running down from the ceiling like a stream of water, with a foam of broken pieces at the bottom. Encased in the purity of this rock was the gleam of gold. Gold, Padre!"

Rivera paused, his breath coming in little gasps. The father had raised himself on one elbow and his eyes fastened intently on the soldier's face. The silence lengthened. At last the weak voice resumed.

"A fever seized my brain, Padre. I was crazed. I rejoined my companions and returned to the encampment, but like one possessed. Gold! I said nothing to my companions but I could think of nothing else. A week passed and we were near Socorro, proceeding up the Rio Bravo, when I could bear it no longer. In the dark of the moon, I slipped out of camp, taking such as I would need and went back to the bowl in the mountains. I stayed there for nearly two years."

The soldier's voice had become fainter and now it ceased. The Father waited for the man to continue, but when he did not, he asked, "What decided you to return to Mexico, my son?"

River sighed. "*Sóledad,* Padre. The loneliness of the great cavern, echoing only to my voice. I have an old mother in Santa Catarina and it came to me that she did not deserve the grief of poverty and neglect from her only son, when I could bring her gold to comfort her declining years."

"*El máno de Diós* touched your heart, *hómbre.* Realizing sin and selfishness is the first step toward repentance. It is never too late to repent or to find the forgiveness of God, amigo."

"No, no. For me, all is finished. Time runs fast. I have not much left. Call it fate, or God, what you will. Fortune turned against me when I found that accursed gold."

"Gold is not an evil," the father said. "It is a part of all the things that are given to us by the good God. It is cursed only when men sin because of it. *Verdád,* you deserted your sworn duty for it, but you left it to return and use it for good. Whatever bad luck befell you was not the fault of the gold."

Silence fell again between the two. Father La Rue's mind

ran over the things the man had told him. If his story were true, the poor soul had come a great distance. Alone and on foot from beyond the great River of the North. Even the caravans of the traders, who came once a year from Santa Fe, had difficulty in making the journey. It was a far distance to the Great River, across hot, desolate plains of the Jornado del Muerto, to the bleached sand dunes of Samalayucca, enduring thirst and the threat of Indians.

"Since you were carried here, you have been too ill for questions. The men found you far from the road, with no water. Surely this was foolish."

Rivera moved his head painfully. "My waterskin was low when I came near the village of Rosario. I would have refilled it there but I was prevented."

"What!" the priest was astonished. "Would no one give you water?"

"A detachment of soldiers was camped on the edge of town," Rivera said, simply. "It would not have been wise to approach. For the same reason, I avoided the highway. I hoped to find a *ciénaga* but all waterholes were dry."

"I see. It has been an unusually dry year. Even the rivers are low." He shook his head, murmuring, "All the way from Rosario, with no water. *Es imposible.*" He stopped, as Rivera's head slipped down on the blanket. Quickly, he bent over the man, feeling for the faint throb of his heart.

"*Pobre viejo.*" He spoke remorsefully. "It was thoughtless of me to keep him talking." He bathed the pale face in cool water and chafed the man's arms and wrists, until the sunken eyes opened.

"Now. That is better. What a fool I am to let you exhaust yourself," he scolded. "Sleep, *hombre*. That is what you need."

Rivera smiled weakly and closed his eyes. When the priest was sure he slept, he rose quietly and went out into the moonlit *placita*. In Magdalena's hut, the women still wailed. Back among the trees, the great house of Don Tomás, its white-washed walls thick as a fortress, shining palely under the moon. Beyond, in the stone corrals, were the vague night sounds of the animals. The Father heard none of these. He was listening to voices of other times and other places. Of the green valley in Spain, where he had been born. The sweet voice of his mother, firm only in her desire to see her son a mitred bishop, and his father equally determined on a brilliant military career for the boy.

He remembered the cool quiet of the mission where he had been educated. The priests liked the boy and he did well in his studies. So well that his father had sent him to Madrid for further learning but, wisely, had omitted to inform the Senora, his mother, that the Academy was for military training. At the end of his first year in Madrid, that call had come for volunteers. Priests and soldiers were needed for service in New Spain. To sail would take him out of the struggle between his mother and his father over the choice of sword or candle and what a chance for high adventure. Everyone knew the wealth of gold and silver to be found in this wild and wonderful new country. Quickly he made his own choice and, in the robes of the Franciscan, he had sailed for Mexico.

Well, the adventure was over, he thought. The fires of his youth had smothered in the heat and sand. He had disciplined his emotions, sternly, to gain wisdom to help the pitifully ignorant people who looked to him for guidance.

Yet the words of the soldier had painted a picture that fanned the faint sparks that still slept in the ashes of his ambition. Father La Rue was human. The thought of the cascade of quartz, glittering with gold, deep in the earth, would have aroused any man's eager interest.

As the priest paced back and forth, his excitement gradually calmed and was replaced by a feeling of deep regret. Regret that this great fortune could be of no use. What good of a treasure, far to the north, that could only be reached across leagues of dry, hot, desert sand?

Yet had he not been praying constantly for deliverance from the hunger, sickness, and poverty brought upon his people by the drought? Could this be the answer? Had the wavering steps of the old soldier been directed toward the hacienda by the hand of God?

He turned toward the little chapel. Prayer. He must approach his God with prayer for understanding. Slowly, his shoulders bowed under the weight of the new responsibility, he entered and knelt, humbly, before the altar.

CHAPTER THREE

Daylight wakened Tirso from the deep sleep of complete emotional exhaustion. His eyes opened and, for a moment, he stared about the room. Then remembrance came, cutting through the mists of sleep. Tears stung his eyes and he sat up, swinging his bare feet to the floor. Dolores was gone but the priest and the old man were stretched near the door.

Grinding his fists into his eyes, he stifled the sobs that rose in his throat. What was he to do now? Never had he felt so small and alone. The finger of fear touched him. No mother, no father, and when Don Tomás returned, he would be moved in with another family who would not look with favor on one more mouth to feed. The house where he had been born would be turned over to others. With mounting dread of the future, he realized that he would have nothing of his own except his blankets and a few things of his mother's.

Looking out at the growing brightness, some words of his father came to him with a calming effect. "Rise, my son, and meet the new day. Forget the mistakes and misfortunes of yesterday. The sun brings everyone a new chance." Getting his hat from the floor, he went out quietly. At the horse trough he ran water over his head, rubbing his face. Smoothing his wet hair, he put on his hat, tucked in his shirt, and squared his shoulders. Today would be a sad one to remember. He wished his father were here to stand at his side.

The little goat must be fed and watered. Tirso attended to that, keeping his eyes averted as he passed the hut where his mother's body lay. In the corral, the goat frisked about his feet as he carried dried grass and piled it in the corner. He brought water from the trough and lingered to stroke her neck while she ate. A sound behind him made him turn his head. A boy of about his own age was leaning over the corral wall.

"*Cómo está amígo.*"

"*Buéno,* Ramon." Tirso got to his feet.

"I am sorry about your mother, Tirso. My father sent me to tell you that breakfast is waiting. We want you to come."

Tirso looked at Ramon, warily. "You are kind," he said. He had learned to be cautious of Ramon's overtures. Since they were old enough to walk, antagonism had flared between these two. Tirso was sober and quiet, keeping to himself most of the time, while Ramon was sly and a little cruel, a leader in the rough horseplay of the other boys.

As the two walked across the *placita* toward Ramon's home, Tirso noted that Ramon's usually insolent eyes were dark with a concealed excitement and he wondered what was going on in the scheming mind of the other boy.

Ramon's home was only a two-room adobe but the walls were clean with whitewash and Señora Lucero's broad, kindly face smiled at Tirso from the fireplace. Hot posole and chile waited to be scooped up on the tortillas which Ramon's sister, Lucia, was cooking. Tirso discovered that he was hungry and thinking back, remembered that he had not eaten since breakfast the morning before. After the meal, he bowed to the Señora.

"*Mil grácias,* for your kindness. I must go now," he said. Ramon followed him outside. Out of earshot of the house, he broke the silence between them.

"*Pués,* Tirso. What did you think of the old man's story last night? Exciting isn't it? What a thing to happen here, where nothing ever happens."

He paused, seeing Tirso's puzzled stare. "What is the matter? You heard him didn't you? You were there at the Father's house. You must have heard the *soldádo* talking about his cave of gold."

Suspicion leaped into his eyes and he seized Tirso's arm, turning him to see his face. "What is this? I see. You and the *Pádre* plan to keep this a secret. To have the gold for yourselves." He stopped again, frowning. Tirso's face was full of puzzled confusion.

"I don't know what you are talking about," he said and Ramon could not but believe the sincerity in his voice. Scorn replaced the anger and suspicion in his eyes.

"*Estupido!* You were right there, where they talked and you hear nothing!" He shook his curly thatch in wonder. "Well, this boy is not so dumb. I went out last night to relieve myself and I heard voices in the Padre's house. So I went closer and listened. The leather-jacket was telling the Father about a place in the north country. He found gold in a cave." Ramon's voice trembled with excitement and his eyes glistened.

Gold! In spite of his distrust of Ramon, Tirso felt the same excitement at his words. Ramon shook his shoulder. "Think of it, slow one. We can all be rich."

Tirso frowned, doubtfully. "I see what is in your mind, Ramon. But I do not think the Padre will favor it. Anyway, we cannot leave the hacienda without the permission of Don Tomás and who knows when he will return from the south."

"True. Nothing can be done without permission." Ramon stopped. Then a thought brought back his smile. "While the *Patrón* is away, Antonio is *mayor-dómo*. Only a word in his ear is required to arrange everything."

"No, no, Ramon," Tirso said hastily. "You must say nothing to Antonio or to anyone until I ask the . . ." He stopped, seeing Ramon's face darken. "That is, I mean, this is a big thing. It requires thought to handle a matter of such magnitude. We must plan cleverly or others will brush us aside and take the credit."

He had hit the right note. Ramon looked at him with new respect. "You are smarter than I thought. It all boils down to a question of whether we lead or follow, no?"

"*Sí*, Ramon. There you have it. *Pués, hómbre,* we need to know much more before we lay our plans. I wonder if *el viéjo* will feel like talking this morning?" He glanced about. "We should not stand here. Already the women are looking at us with curiosity. I will keep an ear open by the sick one. If he so much as whispers, I will hear."

As Tirso hurried toward the little house of the priest, the Father came out into the sunshine, stretching his arms in the bright warmth. Seeing the boy, he called, "Ho, Tirso. You are up. I am afraid I am guilty of a sin. I have been indulging myself with sleep. I was late at my prayers last night, having much on my mind."

"Yes, Pádre." Tirso was respectful. "Shall I make the fire and fix your breakfast?"

"Do so, my son. I am sure you are hungry and, as for myself, I could eat my sandals."

Tirso busied himself getting a fire started and warming tortillas and frijoles. He explained that he had eaten with the Luceros.

"That was kind of Elena," the priest replied. "Push that pot of broth close to the fire. Perhaps the sick one will eat a little, when he wakes."

"There is something which I must tell you, Padre," Tirso said, his eyes turning to the soldier, who still lay quiet, his face drawn and pale. "As you know, I dislike men of his sort. Never have I seen one who was not hard and cruel or who could be trusted. But I must ask. Do you believe his tale of gold in the north?"

La Rue was startled. "*Que páso?* How do you know about the man, Rivera's, story? I thought you asleep. Did you hear?"

"I slept. Ramon told me. He arose in the night and heard you talking to the leather-jacket."

"*Péste!*" The priest struck his hands together. "I would have liked better not to have this known until Don Aránda returns."

"Ramon gossips like a woman. I cautioned him but I think he will brag to the first one he meets."

The priest placed one finger on his chin and thought. "Perhaps I can persuade him to be silent until I can lay the matter before the Patrón."

"Will Don Tomás return soon?" Tirso inquired, dubiously.

"It is uncertain. He mentioned that he might spend the winter in the south."

"Do you think he would be angry, Father, if we went to seek the gold?" Tirso was hesitant. "I do not think Ramon can keep this matter to himself for many months."

"Leave without his consent?" The Father was shocked. "He would most certainly have us all shot." He was pacing up and down, rubbing his hands in distress.

"But if we returned loaded with gold? Would that not please him?"

"Ah, my innocent child," groaned the priest. "Little do you know of the problems involved in this matter."

"But we need the gold, Padre. The storehouses are almost empty. The harvest was small and the tax collectors took much of what we had. With the gold, we would not have to worry about empty bellies."

"So, you think the gold would help." The father's laugh was bitter. "Know you then, that when gold comes into a man's life, peace and contentment fly out. Everyone covets his wealth. The King, the soldiers, even the Church will claim it. Soon we would have nothing."

Tirso regarded him. "You may be right, Father." But he was thinking that gold could not be so very bad. Many things were possible with it. Perhps his mother need not have died if there had been money. Juana, the old *curandéra*, had used her knowledge of herbs without avail, and had told the Father that a cure was impossible because his mother was so weak and thin.

Patting the boy's shoulder, the priest went in to put on his robes and make ready for the funeral rites. Later, as the procession of villagers straggled down from the little cemetery, their thoughts already returning to the details of their lives, Tirso slipped away to his perch overlooking the road north. Up that road lay the wild beautiful country that he had dreamed of so often. And now, the fascination increased as he thought of the story of the old soldier. There was nothing to hold him here at the hacienda. His mother would not need him now. No reason why he could not realize his dreams. Yet, now that it seemed possible, he felt a kind of reluctance. The only friends he had even known were here. What would it be like in a strange country with unfamiliar faces? He sat there until the dusk of evening began to darken the mesas. When, at last, he rose and made his way back to the placita, he saw there was some kind of excitement among the people. The entire village was gathered in front of the padre's home. True to Tirso's guess, Ramon could not keep the luscious plum of knowledge to himself.

The father came from the church and looked gravely at the throng of people. They fell silent and waited expectantly for him to speak. When he did not, they moved restlessly, looking at each other and then back at the priest. Uneasy, under the father's silent, intense gaze, a swarthy fellow in the front rank pulled off his hat and voiced their question.

"Pádre," he said. "we have come to ask you for the truth. This mountain of gold, somewhere to the north, beyond the great river. Is it true?"

A wizened little man pushed in front. "Si, Padre, tell us where we may find these riches of which Ramon speaks."

La Rue's fingers were on his beads. He said reprovingly, "Estevan and you, Andres, speak for the people. But what shall I say to you? I have but risen from my knees, asking God in his wisdom to put the answer in my heart."

Estevan smiled broadly and spread his hands. "Surely, Father, when it is a question of a mountain of gold," he turned to the people and winked, "the only wisdom is to go after it."

Shouts of delighted agreement followed his words.

"Does it seem that simple?" the priest said soberly, looking at the faces turned to him. "In truth, it is almost impossible. And to think of undertaking such a long and perilous journey on only the word of a fever-ridden brain, is preposterous."

Antonio, the *mayor dómo,* moved to stand beside the priest. "Our Padre is right, *amigos.* This is not something to be rushed into and regretted later. It requires thought. Do you think Don Tomás would approve? And if we leave, like mischievous children when his back is turned? Who knows? He could ride after us and have us whipped or even shot for our ill-considered action."

The people looked at each other, doubt spreading. One by one they began to separate and drift toward their homes, talking among themselves. Estevan remained, a scowl darkening his face. "At least let me see the leather-jacket, *Pádre*. I would see for myself what this man has to say."

"Not now, my son," the priest replied. "The soldier sleeps. He is very weak and should not be disturbed. Perhaps, in the morning he can talk with you."

Estevan still scowled, reluctant to leave, until Antonio stepped forward and took his arm. "Come, paisano, let us have a look to see that all is well at the corrals before the night," he said and Éstevan, perforce, went with him.

The father wiped the sweat from his face with his wide sleeve and turned gratefully into the cool walls of his home. Anxiety creased his face and his heart was heavy. Glancing at the thin figure on the cot, he wished fervently that Antonio de Baca Rivera had never come into their lives, bringing this disturbing problem. He bent over the man and touched his forehead. The fever had not returned, but Rivera seemed noticeably weaker. As he watched, the man's eyes opened and he motioned with a slight wave of his hand for the priest to come nearer. His voice was only a whisper as he asked for the last rites. La Rue nodded and prepared himself. Later they talked and, afterward, the soldier seemed relieved and even a little stronger.

In the morning when Dolores came in, the priest left for a while. As he walked through the village, he found most of the women gathered at Elena Lucero's home. Busy making candles for the coming months, their tongues were busier than their hands. As he approached, the talk ceased and the women turned toward him respectfully.

"A good morning, warm and sunny. How does your work progress, my children?"

The women genuflected and chorused, "Very well, Father."

Elena said, "The fat is not of good quality, Father. The animals were very thin. But I think the candles will be adequate."

La Rue moved on, after some conversation, aware of a constraint among the women. He knew their minds were still on Ramon's startling revelation of the night before. It weighed heavily on his conscience that he had not told the villagers the entire truth. Rivera's story had not been told in fevered delirium. His description of the great cave with its glittering wealth had been very clear. And the directions for finding it equally so. The priest knew that he could never erase the soldier's words from his mind. "North on the great highway to the Rio Bravo—cross the river and follow it to a mound of great boulders on the trail—turn to the east toward the rising sun, and cross to the mountains—a canyon will lead to the edge of a great bowl that opens at your feet, with a conical mount rising from its bottom. Under the mount, lies the golden cavern."

The soldier had scratched a rude map in the hard clay floor and knowing that it was printed in his mind, the priest had scuffed it out with his sandal. He groaned. Temptation was of the devil. Reluctantly, he had to admit that the adventurous fires that had burned in him as a youth had been rekindled by Rivera's words. The poverty of the people and the injustices of the Church rankled within him also. The years of struggle had made the Church seem very remote and its officials autocratic figureheads. Yet, let the word of gold come to their ears and they would be swift to punish.

He made his way back to his home and found Dolores on the doorstep, crying. He knew, before she told him, that the soldier was dead. He sighed. At least the villagers would be unable to question the man. Perhaps they would believe that the gold existed only in the imagination of the sick man. If they did not, he trembled to think of the responsibility that would fall on his shoulders.

The feeling on the hacienda was mixed, regarding a burial service for the old soldier. They well knew the cruel, harsh ways of the soldiers of the King and their treatment of the people in the valley, swooping down like vultures, gathering stock, grain, and supplies from the storehouses to satisfy the taxes. Some felt that this soldier was no different and should not be buried with the blessing of the priest. Others said that his mysterious arrival and departure into the unknown was as a spirit from heaven and had brought good fortune into their impoverished lives.

The father, weighing their arguments, said, "It is our responsibility as human beings to see that Antonio de Baca Rivera, Sergeant at Arms, in His Majesty's Army, is buried with full rites for his rank and position."

A grave was dug but outside the wall of the little *cámpo sánto,* the cemetery on the hill. Only a scattering of people attended, as the priest performed the rites of burial.

CHAPTER FOUR

As the days slipped by, the usual serene activity of the hacienda was troubled. The fall work went on. Chili was picked and twisted into long ropes to be hung in the sun, turning scarlet as it dried. Corn was husked and stored—some for winter feed for the animals, some to be piled in the corner of the big storeroom for meal. The dry bean vines were brought in from the field. The brown beans were shaken from the pods, then tossed in a blanket to let the wind blow the chaff away, sacked and hauled into the storehouse. Soon the red strings of chilli would be joined by strings of red beef, cut thin and hung to dry for winter stews. Other meats would be smoked or salted. Ordinarily, this was a time of cheerful smiles and banter, of practical joking and laughter. This year, the people moved silently about the tasks, their minds on the decision before them.

When the evening fires were lit and the villagers came together, talk inevitably moved to the subject uppermost in their minds, the great cavern of gold in the northern country. Emo-

Seven Was the Padre's Number   47

tions varied. Desire, tinged with greed and the wonder of great good fortune had come into their simple lives. Underneath, however, there was fear. Fear of this thing that had upset their tranquil routine of living.

Ramon was in his glory. Swaggering about the *placita* he was pressed to tell and re-tell his story and, with each telling, the size of the cavern and the richness of its treasure increased. The younger men trailed after him, listening and questioning, gold fever sparkling in their eyes. The cautions of the older ones of the village fell on deaf ears. The father warned of the risks and tried dutifully to dissuade the hot-heads from the venture. But in his heart the warm excitement of his youth stirred. Adventure beckoned beyond the horizon to the north, the same urge that had brought him to the shores of Mexico. He knew that his words lacked conviction and he sternly rebuked himself. These tantalizing visions were evil, inspired of the devil.

The morning sun beat warm on Tirso, leaning on the low wall in front of his home. About the placita, the life of the hacienda moved under his somber eyes. Jesus and Antonio emerged from the corrals arguing, caught up their horses, and rode off. Maria, wife of Jesus, stirred a kettle of ill-smelling soap over the fire outside her house. A group of women stopped to chat and their voices came to him on the morning breeze. Tia Anna sat on her doorstep, shelling corn into a basket to be ground into meal for tortillas. In the Lucero home, Elena was scolding Ramon and Tirso grinned. For once Ramon was getting what he deserved. He could not distinguish the words, but her tone left no doubt that she was angry with her son. A voice called and he turned his head to see Lucíta's slender figure, the sun gleaming on her bright hair, skipping toward him. Plopping down, crosslegged at his feet, she twisted her head up to face him with an impish grin.

"*Pués,* my sober friend, what is on your mind this morning?"

The boy shrugged and slid down to squat beside her. Frowning, he said, "It is the question that is on the minds of all. To go north or not."

"*Amigo,* surely you are decided. All you have talked about

is 'When I go north!' That is all I have heard from you for years."

"*Verdád,* Lucíta. It is true that I have long wished to go to the new country. And now comes a chance and I think, what luck. But the Pádre says it is wrong and foolish. Why? Why is it wrong? Is it a bad thing to have plenty to eat and money in the pockets?"

Lucíta bobbed her head in agreement. "It does not seem so to me. Perhaps a new skirt, also." She smoothed her faded, patched skirt over her bare knees. "Ramon is going. He says he will buy me dresses of shiny silk, like those Don Tomás buys for the Señora." She glanced slyly at the boy from under her lashes.

Tirso withdrew into himself and his eyes narrowed. "What you and Ramon do is your own business," he said shortly.

Lucíta laughed, delightedly, "Ah Tirso. Admit it! You are jealous!" she teased. "Would you tear Ramon's gifts from my back?" She considered, her eyes mocking him.

"No. I do not think so. That would be Ramon's way. You would only walk away, with your nose in the air, as if you did not care."

Tirso got to his feet with dignity but the girl caught his hand. "Don't be cross, Tirso. Listen! If they go north, I go too."

"Don't be foolish, Lucíta," Tirso answered, scornfully. "You cannot go with the men. Stay here till we return."

"I am going," she persisted. "If my father goes, my mother and I will go. *Pués,* do you think I want to stay behind like a baby? No! I want to see the country that you talk about. And I shall dig—gold for myself. Who knows? You might not return."

There was talk and more talk. Occasionally tempers flared. At last, the priest, realizing the dissension was leading to trouble, called a council. A great fire was built in the center of the placita and the people gathered round it, the men in front and the women behind them.

The father came into the circle quietly. With the eyes of all fastened on his face, he held out his hands to them in a gesture of appeal. The people waited for him to speak, their faces sullen.

His eyes roved from one to another about the circle, seeking words to reach them.

At last he said, "My children, how can I convince you that it is a grave mistake to undertake this hazardous journey? To leave the peace and security of the hacienda for the glitter of unknown rewards. Think of your wives and children. And you younger men. Do you not owe something to your mothers and fathers now that they are aging and feeble?"

A voice at one side shouted, "The loads of gold we will bring back will comfort them, Father."

"But if you do not return? Who will care for them then?" the priest retorted. "Many have left their bones on the terrible sands of Samalayucca and the waterless waste beyond, which is appropriately named Jornado del Muerto, journey of death."

"Hardship and danger spice the sweetness of the rewards at the end of the journey," said Juan Jose, a heavy, bearded man.

"Juan Jose, how will you answer the *militáres* if they ask your authorization for being on the road? Caravans must have permission," the priest said.

A rumble of voices broke out as the men discussed this point. After a minute the priest went on. "They will throw you in jail and no one will ever see you again. It has happened for lesser crimes."

Andres Lucero said, "Father, I have a thought. Could you not lead us north? We could establish a church. *Por los Índios.* The military would agree that our mission was important if you told them we were going to build a church for the Indians."

"A mission would require papers of authorization from the Church, my friend. Would you wish to wait for months, perhaps years, for such authority to arrive?"

A grumble of dissent answered him. Pablo, a small man, whose hands were busy braiding a quirt, looked up at the priest. "Father, there must be a way. I shut my eyes and I can see the shine of the gold that waits in the mountains. Ah, it is a beautiful sight." His wizened little face twisted into an ecstatic grin.

"Pablo, how can I make you understand? Many things

shine in the fevered mind of a sick man. I believe that the soldier, Rivera, found a mine but I am very doubtful that his description was accurate." He turned again to the men around the fire. "And even if we find the mine and it is as Rivera said, of what value would the gold be to you, staked out on an Apache fire? Or rotting in a jail?"

"When you put it like that, Pádre, it does not sound so good," Pablo grimaced.

"*Aý de mí,*" groaned Estevan, a tall *vaquero*. "It is true. Under Indian attack, we would be helpless."

Ramon's father spoke, thoughtfully, with a sidelong glance at the priest. "The Patron has guns in the big house."

"They are not ours," the father said, quickly.

Estevan's face brightened. "*Sí!* But do you not remember, *Pádre?* When the Apaches came to Chihuahua two winters back? Don Tomás had Antonio pass the guns to each of us so that we might protect the haciénda if they came here?" He looked at Antonio for corroboration. Antonio nodded, glancing at the father's sober face.

"*Sí.* It is true," he said slowly.

Talk burst out again. With guns and a few oxen, which surely Don Tomás would grant them in such a cause, the men felt that success was assured. The priest tried in vain to be heard above the clamor of voices. At last, he threw up his hands and sat down, folding his robe over his knees to keep it out of the dust. He listened but his thoughts ran ahead of the talk. It was evident that nothing would deter the enthusiastic younger men from following the lure of a glittering fortune. How well he could see into their minds and hearts. Theirs was no altruistic goal to bring a better life to those of the haciénda. His lips twisted sardonically. Gold, to them, meant fine clothes, wine, brandy, and all things that went with the fleshpots of high living. But the plausible words that spilled from their lips were sweeping away the better judgment of the older, wiser heads in the village.

Antonio came to stand beside him. "*Pádre,*" he said, "someone must lead. A cool head is needed to organize and give the orders. Someone with authority. These loud-mouths! Pah!" He spat into the dust. "They would have us rush out at daybreak to begin a long journey that will require careful preparation or—" he shrugged, "disaster."

"You speak truth, my son," the priest nodded. "Enthusiasm is an excellent driver but it must be backed by wisdom and caution."

Antonio went on. "I have traveled the road north to Paso del Norte. I carried a message from Don Tomás to a man of money in Paso."

"That is good news," the priest nodded. "Then you know the road."

"It is a long one and hard," Antonio said. He looked impatiently at the clatter around the fire. "The miles of deep sand at Samalayucca will dry up their enthusiasm. Their tongues will be hanging out and their arms will be pulled from the sockets before we get the heavy carts through to the river."

The priest rose and settled his robe. "This," he gestured at the milling, chattering men, "will go on all night. I have some meditating to do before I talk to them in the morning. I will see you then."

Retiring to the chapel, the Father spent most of the night praying for guidance. Early in the morning he sent for Antonio. When the burly *mayor-dómo* appeared, he noted that while the priest appeared pale and worn, there was a serenity and peace on his face.

"It is not a light thing that we attempt, my friend. We are entering upon an effort that will tax the energy of all, even the strongest and may cost us our lives."

Antonio nodded. "*Sí, Pádre.* I take it that you have come to a decision."

The priest sighed. "My knees are black and blue and my brain swims. But I have decided, right or wrong, to attempt this journey and may God in his mercy guide us."

Antonio's eyes lit up. "I am glad. Perhaps the decision will settle my stomach and take the sour taste from my mouth with action."

"You will be in charge, Antonio. I have no experience in such matters. You will also have the difficult task of selection. Only the sturdiest can be allowed to embark on this venture. It will be hard enough without the drag of sick and weak persons to delay us."

For days, the village was in an uproar of preparation as everything was readied for the emigration north. Antonio was a stern and efficient manager. Seldom were his orders and decisions questioned, although there was grumbling among those who would be left behind.

The priest spent several hours and much thought in composing a letter to be left for Don Aránda, explaining the situation that had arisen with the unfortunate words of the dying soldier, the dilemma he had found himself in and what, of necessity, he had decided. He did not put down the location of the mine, saying merely that they hoped to return before word reached the authorities of the Church, for they would surely bring serious charges against him, as well as confiscating any treasure brought back to the hacienda. Ending with his respects and the hope that Don Aránda would view this venture with understanding and compassion, he signed the letter. Then he rolled it and tied it securely, carefully covering the knot with hot wax and stamping it with his seal.

The next day a mounted messenger arrived. Riding from the south, the man had come by the hacienda to leave word that Don and Dona Aránda would spend the winter in Mexico City, returning in April or May, and adding a few instructions for Antonio. The priest calmly fed the man and sent him on his way, saying only that things were going smoothly at the hacienda and that, God willing, they would see Don Aránda in the spring. He did not send the letter. Much could happen in the months before Don Tomás returned. Better that he know nothing of their plans, for the present.

At last they were ready. The father spent the last night in his chapel, praying for God's care and guidance on this journey. In the morning with the first light, he held a mass with a benediction for those who were staying and those who were going. There was some wailing from the women and grumbling from the men, but the almost feudal loyalty of the people for their Patron quieted their feelings. Someone must look after the hacienda until Don Tomás returned.

The little caravan was ready to start. Twenty men and fourteen women were going. Lucíta was accompanying her parents and Dolores had refused to leave the father. Ramon and Tirso had Antonio's consent and the two Cruz boys, Juaníto and Andrés, were old enough to gain his approval, to accompany their father, Beltrán. Señora Cruz had been in poor health so she was to remain with the younger ones. Ramon's sister, Lucia, was to stay to care for her grandmother. Three oxen-drawn carts carried supplies, tools, skins of water, and canvases. Antonio rode his own horse and a mule had been provided for the father. The rest were prepared to walk with their few personal possessions rolled in blankets on their backs.

The priest had thought two carts sufficient but Antonio over-ruled him.

"We will travel faster, without the danger of breakdowns in over-loaded carts. And remember, Padre, we hope to bring back gold and gold is very heavy."

CHAPTER FIVE

Few slept on the eve of their journey and the first rays of the morning sun found the caravan readying to move out. Lucíta's bright hair gleamed like a torch, as she waited near the front of the column. She felt the warmth on her thin shoulders but her hands were icy with nervous excitement and she hugged herself, dancing a little jig of impatience.

"*Por Diós,*" she said to Tirso who stood near. "Why do we wait? Everyone is ready. Every strap has been buckled and every rope knotted. What remains to be done?"

"Patience, *niña,*" Tirso replied. "Antonio and the Padre are riding to the front now. I think they are about to give the signal."

Even as he spoke, the priest's arm went up and the column

began to move. A fresh outburst of wailing rose from the women and the cries of *"adiós, adiós,"* "God be with you," followed them. The great gates of the hacienda swung open and the line of men and women, with the ox-drawn carts bringing up the rear, trailed through and turned north.

The sky was clear with a promise of heat in the hours to come. The father and Antonio rode at the head of the straggling line, with the wheels of the heavy carts grinding the dust in an agony of sound.

"God knows the Indians cannot be unaware of our company, Padre," Antonio observed. "They can hear us for leagues."

"Let us hope that their evil business takes them far from here," the priest answered.

To the west, the blue Sierra Madres blended with the color of the sky. Between the column and the mountains were the broken outlines of the foothills, greenish grey with mesquite and chaparral. The father wondered if the country ahead would look the same. Up in the hills were the fierce Tabosa and Tarahumara Indians, savages who had never bowed to the rule of Spain. Unaffected by the sporadic forays of the soldiers, they ranged the country, living in caves in the mountains, resisting every effort by the military and the Church to civilize them. The priest spoke of this to Antonio, who nodded.

"All Indians are bad, Padre, but the devil Apaches from the north are the worst. This is the season when they sweep down along the Rio Bravo and south, raiding, killing, and burning." He shivered. "If they find us, pray that you get an arrow through your throat and die quickly."

The road climbed, winding up to the top of a low ridge and the two pulled aside and waited for the line to catch up.

Antonio pointed back. "This will be the last sight of the hacienda, Padre," he said.

The priest's eyes followed his gesture, past the toiling ox-carts to the buildings of the hacienda grouped on the crest of a little rise. The sun shone on the roofs and sparkled on the thread of silver that was the Rio Chuvíscar. Above the trees that shaded the village, the thick-walled shape of Casa Aránda showed and near it, the white steeple of the little chapel lifted bravely. The yellow fields, dotted with cattle and sheep now that the crops were in, spread to the foothills. As he looked at the serenity and peace that they were leaving, a premonition chilled him, a feeling that never again would he enter the gates of the hacienda or see his chapel and his friends. So strong was this feeling that he glanced at Antonio to see if the stocky *mayor-dómo* shared it. Antonio's face was gloomy as he watched the slow progress of the column.

"Padre," he said. "I think we must be mad. To leave this security for what? A possibility of riches but an even greater possibility of death."

The line had come up and was passing, the oxen with their heads set stiff-necked, shoving at the yokes. The priest looked at the faces of his band. Stolid determination marked the older ones, their minds made up. A few paused to look back at the home they were leaving but there was no indecision. The younger members were gay, joking as they walked. This was their big adventure. He sighed. The mule turned its head and eyed the priest as if to ask why they were delaying and he lifted the reins to move on.

"Come, Antonio. The die is cast and whatever the Lord has in mind for our future, our course must be north." The mule jerked its head and moved forward. "Even Pardo, my mule, knows that the past is better left behind."

Curious glances followed the band as they came to the outskirts of Chihuahua. Wanting to avoid notice, the priest led them around the edge of the city, although the women cast longing eyes at the busy streets and shops. A few men and women, pausing in their work, smiled and called as the caravan passed. Then they turned onto the broad Camino Réal and Antonio nodded to the priest with a smile of relief.

"*Está buéno,* Padre. I do not think anyone knew us."

"*Sí*, Antonio. Luckily none of our friends from the city were about. And the farther we go, the less danger of recognition."

The highway wound steeply up from the city and the white clouds in the west were flaming above the purple-cloaked mountains before the oxen labored to the top. Pulling well off the road, Antonio selected a place to camp, far enough to discourage visitors. A tiny spring, dammed by rocks, formed a pool. The oxen were unspanned and staked out for the night and the stock was hobbled so they could not stray far. Cook fires sprang up and the women busied themselves preparing food.

Dolores, going to the spring for water, saw Tirso leaning against an outcrop of rock, his eyes on the lights of Chihuahua that sparkled in the distance. He looked so alone, standing quietly in the fading light, contrasted to the cheerful chatter and laughter among the camp fires, that her heart went out to him.

She set down her olla and went to him, slipping a small hand into his. "I know how you feel, Tirso. I too am sorry to leave familiar things and friends. But are you not glad also? Seeing new country and, when we return to the hacienda, bringing the happiness of wealth to our people!"

Looking at her face, flushed with the reflected light of the sunset, Tirso's mood lightened. He smiled into the dark eyes so near his own.

"To exchange the familiar for the unknown is a little fearsome." He paused. "I am not *un cobárde,* Dolores. The new country has long called to me with a fascination that I cannot explain. But the uncertainty makes me wonder. What will we find? How will things go with us?"

Dolores's quiet face broke into one of her rare smiles. "Ah, Tirso. Do not worry about what is ahead. When is the future ever certain? We will do what we must, whenever the time arises. And we have the Padre and Antonio to guide and help us."

Tirso returned her smile. "You speak the truth, Dolores. You and I are alike in that we are alone, with no father or mother to guide us. But the Padre will not let us fail."

Dolores nodded. "Since the smallpox took my parents, the good father has taken their place. I trust him as I do no other. I know that he doubted the wisdom of this venture. Yet I know that he sympathizes with the people. I have heard him praying that God will keep him from the sins of the love of gold."

"I too trust him. He has never failed me when I needed help. As for the sin of loving gold, it can bring much good."

"Come and share our fire," the girl said. "I have food nearly ready for the Padre." She lifted the olla from beside the spring and they walked to the camp, companionably.

Lucíta watched with sultry eyes and strolled across to Tirso while Dolores was busy.

"Very cozy," she said mockingly. "You and the little dove alone by the water pool. What will the father think?"

Tirso returned her look cooly. "Nothing, you little witch, but it is evident what is in your mind. Calm yourself. We but talked for a few minutes. Why should that upset you?"

"I am not upset," Lucíta said scornfully. "It is nothing to me what you do. It is a pity that we could not have camped near Chihuahua. Ramon wants to ride down and dance awhile."

Tirso looked at her sharply. "That would be foolish. A drink or two and he would be telling all who would listen about our plans."

Lucíta saw Dolores approaching with a well-filled pan from the fire. She dug her nails into his arm and hissed, "See that you do not tell, *amigo*." Then she was gone.

Antonio strolled over to the priest after the meal. "The stock is cared for and hobbled, Padre. We must be up and gone by daylight. There will be a moon tonight and I think a guard had better be set."

"Since the men are tired and I have been riding all day, I will watch," the priest said.

"I too, Padre. I will share the hours."

"Then let me take the first watch," the priest proposed. "I have difficulty in getting to sleep and will welcome the chance to be of use. There is little of the work I can do on the trail."

The father held a short ceremony of benediction and prayer and the camp settled down. Blanket-wrapped forms lay near the fire. The only sounds were the movements of the animals and the heavy breathing of the tired sleepers. Folding his blanket about him, he sat down to watch the slow climb of the moon emerging above the horizon. As the silence deepened, he became aware of a murmur of voices from beyond the pool. He listened. In a little while the voices became clearer and he realized that it was an argument. He rose and moved quickly across the intervening space. As he passed the pool, he saw them. Two figures facing each other like fighting cocks. Ramon and Tirso were glaring with eyes bright with anger.

"*Que páso, hijos?*" the priest demanded. Tirso turned his head, his eyes never leaving Ramon's face.

"This need not concern you, Padre. A matter which Ramon and I will settle between us."

Ramon spoke hotly. "It is settled, or will be when I speak to the Señora, Lucíta's mother. Think you she will favor a homeless orphan without a *péso* to his name to one whose family owns a cart and five cows? A good start on future herds? The Señora Rosa is not a fool."

"Does the possession of five cows also give you the right to tell me who I shall walk and talk to? *Pués*, the girl has a mind of her own. From what I have seen, she does not dance to your tune or any others." Tirso's eyes were flashing.

Father La Rue's eyes were stern. "This is something we cannot have. Quarreling among ourselves. As Tirso says, Lucíta divides her favors as she pleases. But this expedition is too important to all to have personal quarrels among ourselves. The dangers and hardships which lie ahead of us demand that we stand together, with an undivided front to our enemies. If I cannot be assured of this, I shall turn back to the hacienda at once."

The threat was effective. The priest had not revealed to anyone their exact destination. He alone knew the route that the soldier had marked out. Tirso was quickest to grasp the father's meaning.

"The Padre is right, Ramon. The matter between us must be settled after we reach the *mína del óro*. Who knows," there was a grim twinkle in his eye, "perhaps my fortune may be better then."

Ramon, still angry, turned and strode off to his blankets. The priest sighed and shook his head. Tirso turned to him, the moonlight shining on his face. "Forgive me, Padre. I do not mean to make things harder for you. I will try to avoid any more trouble, but believe me, with Ramon, it will not be easy."

As the father returned to his place, Dolores pushed back her blanket and came to sit beside him. Her dark eyes were large in the face she turned up to him.

"*Por amór de Diós,* Padre," she said. "What can be done between these two? There has been rivalry and sometimes words have been said, by one or the other, but to come to blows. It is not good. Can you not stop this foolishness before it becomes real enmity?"

"I hope so, *nína*. I shall try. They are young and impulsive. At an age when what one does, the other must do better."

"You cannot really say that Tirso is impulsive, Padre. Ramon, yes. He brags and blows and thinks only of his importance. But Tirso is so thoughtful and considerate. He is worth a hundred Ramons."

The priest looked at her, thoughtfully. "You think a great deal of Tirso, my dear. Is it not so?"

The girl's head drooped and long lashes veiled her eyes.

"Yes, father," she said softly.

The priest reached over and patted her hand. "Do not worry, I will say nothing about this. But you know you have my blessing. Tirso is a fine boy."

Dolores thought of Tirso, his dark head bent over hers, as they talked beside the pool. His words, "we are two of a kind" and his hand on hers, brought a sweet weakness in her. Was it that his interest was stirring? Her heart lifted, then sank. Perhaps it was only kindness. Tirso was always kind. If only Lucíta had not come with the caravan, she felt sure that she could win him. A long sighing breath escaped her.

The priest was watching her. "What troubles you, *niña?*"

"Nothing of importance, Padre."

The father thought he knew the answer. Lucíta. A lovely girl with a magnetic personality and fire that made the other women seem dull and colorless. Dolores was lovely too, but her beauty was cool as a mountain spring. Her shyness kept her in the background, while Lucíta, glowing and full of life, was the center of all eyes. There was a saying about women of their race, beautiful at eighteen, ripe at twenty, withered by thirty. Both girls were like ripening buds. He foresaw trouble ahead in Lucíta's flashing eyes and provocative ways. Glancing again at Dolores, he saw that she slept but the moonlight showed the marks of tears on her cheeks.

Antonio's roar awakened the camp, well before dawn. Fires were rekindled and, while the women prepared food, the men brought up the stock and the oxen were hitched to the carts and the waterskins—checked for leaks and filled under the watchful eye of the burly *mayor-dómo*.

"There will be a dry camp tonight," he warned, "and perhaps for several nights. Water is scarce in the leagues between us and the Rio Bravo."

As they moved out onto the road, the father looked back. The camp fires glowed dully in the semi-dark. Far behind, a few lights of early risers in Chihuahua twinkled faintly. Ahead was a wilderness of unknown dangers, heat, thirst, and Indians.

That night, as Antonio had predicted, they found no water. The next night and the next were no better. The supply of water dwindled and the little caravan toiled along, day after day, in a fog of strangling dust. The solid wood wheels of the heavy carts gouged deep into the silty soil. The precious water was doled out in dipperfuls, the oxen getting a small ration at night and morning, the people a swallow from time to time.

On the morning of the fifth day, Antonio encouraged them.

"*Brávo, hómbres!* You have done well. Tonight we should be near Lago Enciníllas and there will be water for all. One more day, *amígos*. The road lies along the shore of the lake and three days travel beyond, we should reach the Rio Carmen. The worst is over. *Vámos al nórte,* brave ones."

By sundown, the desert still stretched ahead but suddenly the mule pricked up its ears and quickened its steps. Antonio called out, "Hola! The lake must be near. The animals smell water." In a half hour, the lake, red in the setting sun, came into view.

The stock plunged ahead to get to the water. Men and women broke into a run. The wheels of the oxcarts shrilled as the oxen quickened their pace, shuffling their big splay feet on the downward slope to the lake. Suddenly the dun ox, Cisco, lurched to its knees and the sickening sound of bone cracking startled the driver. The ox came up at once, but its left front leg dangled loosely. Juan Jose dropped his pole and knelt to examine the injured ox, already knowing the consequences. Then he rose and shouted to Antonio. Fernandez and Estevan guided their carts around the stalled vehicle and stopped. Antonio rode back, his face a mask of dust. "*Que páso, hómbre?*"

Juan Jose lifted his shoulders and spread his hands. "They smelled the water and I could not hold them. Cisco stepped in a hole. That is how it happened. The leg is broken." He shrugged again fatalistically.

"*Por Diós!* This is a bad thing. The ox must be destroyed." Antonio turned and called to one of the men. "Vénga aqúi, Pedro. Get the head straps off this animal and put another in its place. The poor beast must be shot. We will cut meat for the camp and leave the rest for the wolves."

With some difficulty, the stock was driven from the water and moved a mile or so north along the lake where camp was made. Antonio walked to the stricken ox which was bawling in pain and shot it. The men stripped off the hide and cut chunks of meat from the carcass to be divided among the cook pots.

That night sleep was fitful and the sleepers were restless. The sounds of the wolves, fighting among themselves over what remained of the carcass, could be heard from the camp.

CHAPTER SIX

In the morning the camp was moved to the far side of the lake, away from the road. Lago Encinillas was five miles or more in width and stretched for twenty miles, north and south, along the Camino Réal. The father wished to stay away from other travelers and curious questions. The stock was staked out to graze in the grass which grew luxuriantly near the lake shores and the women were soon knee deep in the water, washing the trail dust from piles of soiled clothing.

Dolores, soaping and beating a blanket, watched a little jealously as Lucíta washed her hair. It was just the color of the beaten copper urn that stood in the doorway of Dona Aránda's home. From a little distance away, the sounds of splashing and shouts came from beyond an upthrust of rocks where the men were swimming. Churning water was splintered by sleek bodies appearing and disappearing in the foam. Lucíta shook her wet hair back, pouting.

"Men have all the fun," she exclaimed. "They swim and dive while we wash dirty clothes."

Her mother looked at her, ironically. "Much work you do, *muchacha*. The men have finished their tasks and when we are done here, we will bathe."

Lucíta scowled. "I still say the men have more fun. Why can we not swim as they do, not bundled in clothes, splashing water on each other like children?"

Elena Lucero looked up with a gasp. "Bathe mother-naked like the men? It would be a disgrace. What are you thinking of, child?"

Lucíta's mother frowned, disapprovingly. "I shall speak to the Padre, Lucíta. I think he must have a talk with you."

The other women had stopped their work and stared open-mouthed at Lucíta. They shot glances at each other, rolling their eyes in horror. Rosa cast an angry look at the girl. Before she could speak, Dolores broke in. Placing her hands on her back, she straightened up painfully. "*Mádre mía!* This washing kills me. Lucíta, help me carry this blanket to the grass to dry."

Lucíta tossed back her hair and threw her a thankful smile. The girls carried the blanket up the sloping bank and stretched it in the sun. Dolores sank down on the grass and stretched tired muscles. Lucíta joined her.

"*Pués, muchácha,* you spoke just in time. Another moment and the women would have been on me like dogs on a bone. I do not think what I said was so bad."

"They are tired," Dolores said gently. "When we are clean and rested, they will not be so cross."

"Work, work and walk and walk. Will we never get to the end of it?" Lucíta complained.

"There is much more to come," Dolores admitted. "Antonio told the Padre last night that we have more desert ahead, after we leave the lake. But think how wonderful it will be when we reach the mountain. We will fill the bags with gold and return to the hacienda. Then, no more work. We can hire Indian girls to wash and cook."

"I shall not stay at the hacienda," Lucíta declared. "I am going to Mexico City and live like a lady." She tossed her head. "Ramon says that gold will buy many things. Jewels and silks to wear and a nice house. I do not intend to stay and be ordered about by Don Tomás."

Dolores shook her dark head. "The Padre returns to the hacienda and I shall stay with him. I can never repay the debt I owe him. I was a small orphan. Others were kind but the Padre took me in and gave me a place in his home. He loved me and taught me as he would a daughter. I will never leave him as long as he needs me."

Lucíta looked at her curiously. "*Pués,* girl. you are too pretty to spend your life taking care of a priest. Those black eyes could set men on fire, if you tried. With a bag of gold, you could have any man in the country at your call."

"But I do not wish to set any one on fire, Lucíta," Dolores protested. She thought of Tirso and felt the blood creep into her cheeks.

Lucíta laughed. "Aha. Does a kitten not like cream? I do not intend to grow old and fat without tasting some of the fun in life. What good is it to be young and pretty if you do not have fun?"

Dolores, still flushed, rose to her feet. "Look. The women have finished and are already going to bathe. Hurry. Let us go."

The respite of the lake was like a holiday. Moving slowly, they made only a few miles each day, enjoying the cooler air. At night, Juan Jose and Ramon brought their guitars to the fire for singing and dancing. Everyone was gay and none more so than Lucíta. She drew attention wherever she was, twirling in the colorful dances, flirting extravagant glances at the men, laughing with the women over the gossip at the fires. Tirso had made up his mind to take her for a stroll along the lakeshore but when he looked for her she was gone. Her mother shrugged her shoulders when he asked.

"She asked no permission," Rosa told him. "One minute she was here. The next, she was gone."

"Never mind, Señora," Tirso said. "I will find her for you."

He thought perhaps she had slipped away and was waiting for him in the darkness. He made his way to the lake and looked up and down along the shore, hoping for a glimpse of her. A shadowy movement caught his eye and he followed it quickly. He was about to call out when he heard the low murmur of voices. Soundlessly, he moved closer until he knew that she was with Ramon.

His face was dark and angry as he returned and went to his blankets. He lay wide-eyed in the darkness, hating Ramon, hating himself. Why could he never do things quickly and easily, like Ramon? Always, Ramon did things while he was still thinking about them. Dolores, too, was awake. She had seen Ramon and Lucíta slip away and, later had watched with compassion as Tirso followed and then returned, his heavy tread betraying his anger. She wished she could do or say something comforting, but it would only hurt his pride to let him know that she knew. Above them, the stars twinkled in millions of tiny points of light and a cool breeze brushed their faces. A night bird cried from the lake and the murmur and slap of the water lulled them. In a little, they fell asleep.

This was their last night at Lago Encinillas. The next morning, water skins filled, rested and refreshed, they turned again into the sand and cactus of the desert. A big red ox had taken the place of Cisco. An ill-tempered brute, it seemed determined to cause as much trouble as possible. Juan Jose belabored the animal with his pole and cursed the ill luck that had lost him Cisco.

"*Arre buéyes! Estúpido!* Cisco was worth ten of your mangy

hide." He strode beside the cart, its wide wheels screeching a dry duet, leaving broad tracks in the sand. Behind him the other two carts followed, Estevan and Fernandez grinning.

"Our *compádre* is in a bad humor this morning," Fernandez commented.

"It will pass," Estevan replied. "The red one is strong. A few days on the trail and he will settle down."

Strung out behind the carts, the people moved slowly, watching to see that the stock did not wander far. Grey thickets and dull green cactus grew in patches across the bare mesas, with occasional boulders, jutting like weatherbeaten bones, washed down from the ragged upthrusts of the hills to the west. The wind came as the sun moved up into the sky, bringing a veil of dust.

So far, they had met no other travelers. Now they saw a line of loaded burrows approaching, roped together behind a mule-drawn cart, its cargo carefully covered and lashed down. Six men rode alongside the carts, casting curious glances at the colony as they passed. Slumped with fatigue, they did not offer to stop.

Antonio took off his hat and mopped the sweat from his face. "Ahé, Padre! It is good that those *viajéros* did not wish to talk."

"Very good," the padre replied. "Their business must be urgent. From their appearance it would seem that they had traveled all night."

"Their water skins were hanging limp," Antonio worried. "There are four dry camps ahead to the Rio Carmen. I hope their haste does not mean that we will find its course dry."

Burning heat of days, dust and glare, chill of nights, doggedly the little caravan plodded on. As the sun lowered on the fifth day, Antonio rode ahead and turned down the flinty wash of the Rio Carmen. Dismayed, he found not even a trickle of water showing on the gravelly bed. He rode first up and then down the dry course, looking for puddles on the low places. Then he sat down to wait for the others.

The ox-carts pulled up and the oxen stretched their necks

toward the dry wash, bawling their anxiety and thirst. The padre slid from Pardo's back and stood with the men, concern on his face.

"How much water do we have, Antonio?" he asked.

"Very little, Padre." Discouragement was in the foreman's voice.

Disappointment was turning to anger among the others, as they took in the situation. Hot, thirsty, and grimy they looked for something or someone to blame. Antonio seemed the logical one and they turned on him with bitter remarks. Silent against the angry words, Antonio knew that to try to answer them, to point out that he had warned them of the hardships to be met, was useless. He knew that the outpouring was resentment born of the heat and their fatigue, rather than at himself. After a little, the clamor died down as one after another sat down to stare at the dry riverbed, dejected and spent.

Tirso pulled at the Father's sleeve and pointed. "*Mira, Padre!* Look at Pardo!"

The mule had moved down the wash, sniffing the gravel and now he was pawing the rocks aside. Juan Jose and Pedro jumped to their feet and hurried to the animal's side. Then came Pedro's shout. "The earth is damp. Bring shovels! We must dig here."

Eagerly the men rushed to cut away the dirt and as the hole deepened, water began to seep into the bottom. By sunset, enough water had been dipped out to fill one of the big pots to settle for the camp. Afterwards, the stock was watered, two at a time and hobbled for the night. Pardo was the first to be led to the hole and he pushed his nose down into the water, sucking noisily. The priest patted his grizzled neck and rubbed his ears.

"Good boy, Pardo," he said. "We should make you second-in-command with Antonio. Such wit and good sense deserves a reward."

The mule lifted its grey head and shook the drops from its nose. Then it lifted its voice in a loud bray of appreciation and everyone laughed. The tension of disappointment was broken and the men sheepishly apologized, one after another, to Antonio.

"*Náda. Es náda,*" he said gruffly. "Your feelings were to be expected. It has, as I promised you, been a hard journey. Let us hope the rest of the way will be happier."

They found water in low places and sink holes of the Carmen, as they followed its course north for the next two days. Some of the waterskins were replenished by the time the road turned toward the dreaded sands of Samalayucca. If their pace had seemed slow before, it dropped to a crawl once they entered the dunes of soft, deep sand. Every step was an effort. The oxen were doubled and often sank to their bellies. Everyone pushed and the animals strained under the weight of the heavy carts.

El Camino Réal ran straight north across the dunes for ten miles or more, before descending into the valley of the Rio Bravo. Antonio had changed their course, to cross the eastern end of the dunes, cutting the travel through the sands to five miles. These dunes were one of the greatest obstacles of the road. Every year they claimed the lives of travelers in the frequent winds that whirled the sand in blinding clouds that smothered and buried the unwary.

The easterly direction, quartering across to the Bravo, would add miles to their travel but would avoid much of the sand and lessen the likelihood of meeting other parties on the way. By bending every effort, they advanced only two miles in the first long day. The second morning, the wind rose early and by midday was sweeping with such force that they had to turn their heads to breathe.

The wind strengthened steadily and the blasting sand thickened, obscuring their vision. When it became impossible to keep the animals moving, the carts were pulled as close together as possible, the stock roped to keep them from drifting away and the people huddled down in the slight shelter of the carts, pulling their blankets over their heads. Sometime in the night, the wind went down and the first risers looked out on a misty world, veiled by dust that hung in the air, only the faint disc of the sun giving them direction. Bleary-eyed, hawking dust from throats that burned, they stared about at the creamy ripples of sand.

"*Mira!*" Estevan called out. "There is not a track in view.

It is as if we had landed here from the air. Even the deep ruts of our wheels are gone."

"Let's go, *amigos,*" Antonio's roar stirred them to life. "Get the fires going and round up the cattle. They have broken loose."

The stock was scattering to hunt the sparse clumps of sotol. Estevan, Pablo, and Fernandez started out after them. Juan Jose got a waterskin and prepared to ration it out for the animals. Antonio watched him gloomily.

"*Por favór a Diós,* we will be out of this accursed sand by tonight. Let us start as soon as is possible."

Pedro called. "Luisa! Luisa! Where are you? Curse the woman. I am hungry and where is my wife? Snoring her head off without doubt. Luisa!"

There was no answer. Everyone was up, shaking sand from blankets and clothing. They stared at Pedro and around at each other. Rosa said, quietly, at first, "She is not here. Where . . . ?" Her voice trailed away.

Dolores darted to the carts and looked under and around them, then came back to spread her hands, helplessly.

Antonio glanced at the alarm forming in the faces around him. "It is true. she is not among us."

Pedro put a trembling hand to his mouth. "Mother of God! The storm! Where is my Luisa!?"

Elena Lucero put her arm across his shoulder in sympathy, her eyes full of a premonition of tragedy.

Antonio cleared his throat gruffly. "When did she disappear? Who saw her last?"

The women looked at each other and shook their heads.

"With the wind, we covered our heads. The sand hid us as we walked. Everyone was just shapes." Rosa said.

Lucíta's face was white. "*Probrecíta.* We were all exhausted. Perhaps she fell and covered herself. We must look. She may be behind us."

Pedro was walking about aimlessly, peering first one way and then another. Now he sank down and put his hands over his face. "My Luisa. Out there in the storm alone. So small. The wind could whisk her away. Only God knows where she is."

The father was grim. "Antonio, get the men back on the trail. Perhaps we can find her. I blame myself for this accident, I should have watched over you more closely."

"No, Padre," Dolores said swiftly. "You are not to blame. No one could see in that terrible wall of sand. Even if she had called out, her voice would have been lost in the howling of the wind."

Antonio put his hand on Pedro's shoulder. "Come, *hómbre.* Let us go and see what we can find. Perhaps Luisa wanders out of sight of camp."

Lucíta had tears in her eyes. "Yes. Let us hurry. How awful if Luisa got up and could see only emptiness."

"Not you, Lucíta," Antonio said with authority. "The men will go. The women will stay and watch the stock."

The girl ran to Tirso and seized his hand. "Let me go. I cannot sit and wait. I can walk as fast and see as far as any man," she pleaded.

Antonio's sharp "No!" settled the matter. Hobbling the stock, the men moved out into the blank, white wilderness of dunes. After they were gone, the women busied themselves, halfheartedly shaking the dust from blankets and garments. Lucíta flounced down near Dolores and began to brush her hair, its coppery sheen dulled by the dust of the storm.

"I wish I was a boy," she grumbled. "Girls must always stay behind."

"For shame," Dolores reproved. "Do you never think of anyone but yourself? Poor woman, wandering alone out there. She must be terrified. Think also of the Padre. He is torturing himself." Her eyes went to the figure of the priest who had withdrawn some distance and was kneeling in prayer.

The hours dragged on. When the women could think of nothing else to do, they sat in a miserable huddle around a small fire of mesquite roots, watching for the return of the men. Late in the afternoon, Lucíta, who had made frequent excursions to scan the back trail, called out, "They come. I see them."

Every one rushed to stand beside her, peering, none more anxiously than the father, at the distant figures. As the men came closer, doubt became certainty. Luisa was not with them.

The men came in, reeling with weariness, hungry and sweating from hours of plodding through deep sand. Their faces confirmed the bad news. No trace of the missing woman had been found. She had vanished completely. Somewhere in the whirling blizzard of sand, she had ceased to exist.

Pedro sank down and looked up at the priest, his eyes pleading. "Padre, we cannot go away and leave my Luisa without a sign. Could you say the words for death and we will place a marker here where she left us? *Por favor, Padre.*"

"*Sí,* Pedro. Everything shall be done as you wish."

After they had eaten, the father held a solemn mass for the dead. A crude cross was made from pieces from one end of a cart and driven deep into the sand. While the women wailed, Pedro placed a candle beneath it and lighted it. The priest laid his hand on Pedro's shoulder and spoke comforting words.

"Do not lament, my son. Luisa was a good woman. The Lord will take her to be with him and she will never know hunger, cold, or thirst again. We who remain will suffer the pain of living."

Sometime that night, a rain fell, packing the sand and providing water. Travel was easier that day. Pedro lagged at the end of the line, stopping often to gaze behind. Dolores dropped back to walk beside him, her heart wrung at his tormented face. Looking at his broad shoulders, bent now with grief, her thoughts went back to the hacienda. Luisa and Pedro, their home always gay and warm. Luisa calling to her to come in for a cup of chocolate and a chat. Pedro at the fiestas, spinning his slender wife in the *Jarábe*. It was only a few years since she had danced at their wedding.

Pedro's lagging walk had slowed once more to a stop, as he turned to stare back. Dolores's eyes followed his. The white dunes stretched away blank and empty.

"This that has happened is my fault," he said, his face twisting. "I was the one who wanted to be rich and adventurous. I wanted to see new country and fill my pockets with gold. Luisa cared only to make me happy."

"No, Pedro. Do not blame yourself," Dolores protested. "We were all told of the dangers of this journey. We all came, knowing that many forms of death lay in wait along our trail. It was for the gold and the great amount of good that can be done with it for those who wait at the hacienda. If there is blame, we all share it."

She did not know if he heard her words. His eyes were dull and unseeing with grief.

That night they camped on the edge of the bleached sand dunes. Before them the land sloped down, in rocky terraces, to the green valley of the Rio Bravo. Flickering lights in the distant mass of the trees that outlined the course of the river, told them that here were houses and people and the thought lifted their spirits from the tensions and tragedy of the day.

After the simple meal, the father noticed that Pedro was sitting alone, his plate untasted and went to sit beside him. Neither spoke for a time, then Pedro thrust the plate from him and buried his face in his hands.

"Padre, I do not know what to do. I have no desire to go on, to find riches without Luisa. Without my wife, nothing has meaning."

"This is a time of great anguish for you, Pedro," the priest said gently. "But do not say that nothing has meaning. *Grácias a Diós,* who forgives our sins and our mistakes, we live on to find meaning."

Pedro sobbed.

"God does not tell us his reasons why the lot of some men is hard and that of others is easy. Perhaps the hardships make us stronger to meet things still to come." He paused, and then went on. "I believe that having started this matter of gold and having come so far and endured so much, we must go on. Perhaps we will find meaning in the end."

Pedro shook his head. "It does not matter, Padre. If you say it is better to go on, I will go. There is nothing here and no reason to return to the hacienda."

When the priest left him and went to his blankets, he knelt for some time, praying for guidance. Even after he lay down, sleep would not come. His mind was a turmoil of doubt in himself and his motives. Had God directed this journey or was it his own desire for adventure which had led him to take the colony north. A nagging feeling of guilt was at the bottom of his mind. What was he leading these people into? They were like children, believing that his words and deeds were infallibly guided by God. At last, from exhaustion, he slept.

CHAPTER SEVEN

"Three days to the river." Antonio squinted his eyes toward the dark line of the valley. "We will strike it some distance below Paso but it is unlikely that we will encounter unwelcome company."

"*Buéno.*" The father nodded, vigorously. "We want no *militáres* or any others to mark our passing."

The slow crawl of their progress through deep sand and across rough gullies sapped their energies. The gaunt oxen toiled, stumbling more and more often. The pale mounds of the dunes fell behind as they crossed dry flats, white with alkali, that rose from the wheels in acrid clouds, coating their clothing and turning the animals white. Thickets of tornillo raked the carts and tore at their garments, inflicting deep scratches on the unwary.

On the last day, they moved through brush to the edge of the river, pushing themselves past sundown to make camp in the bosque. Shaking with fatigue, a fire was built with rotting limbs of fallen cottonwoods and the men watered and hobbled the stock for the night. Antonio and the priest bent over Pardo who had lamed, examining the bad leg. The mule turned its grizzled head to watch as Antonio prodded and massaged the muscles, working downward. As the foreman got to the hock, Pardo picked up his foot and Antonio, thinking he had hit a sore spot, stepped quickly aside to avoid a lashing response to pain. Pardo wrinkled his nose, baring long yellow teeth, but stood quietly holding his foot up.

"I think he wants you to look at his hoof, *hómbre*," the priest said.

Antonio examined the hoof and then the pad. "*Mira,* Padre. Here is the cause. A stone is embedded next to the shoe. Look how far it is driven in. No wonder it caused him pain." With his knife point, he carefully loosened the rock and lifted it out. Pardo lowered his foot and tested his weight on it. Then, swinging his head around, he bumped Antonio, almost knocking him from his feet and strolled away, his limp gone, to crop the tall grass near the river.

The priest laughed. "Ho, Antonio. Pardo says '*Grácias*'! He is a smart one, that mule."

A cold wind blew down the valley, whistling through the pass between the mountains where the river slipped through. Too exhausted for talk or music this night, the colony rolled their blankets close to the fire and soon dropped into the deep sleep of utter fatigue.

Two figures sat on, the flames of the fire flickering over their faces. The priest put his hand on Pedro's knee.

"My son, you torture yourself beyond reason. Grief is natural. It comes to all. You have good memories of years of happiness. Try to find comfort in these memories. *Así es la vída.*"

"So is life," Pedro repeated dully. "*Porqúe,* Padre?"

"We do not know why, Pedro. Only God knows why these things happen."

Silence fell. Pedro stared into the deepening night. Minutes passed and then the priest said gently, "Pedro, you should get some rest. Sleep so that tomorrow's burdens can be borne."

Pedro shook his head. "I cannot sleep, Padre. Dreams come to torment me. I see Luisa walking, walking in the sand. Struggling in the wind. Calling to me for help. Then I waken and it seems so real that I must rush back to find her. Tell me, Padre, are these dreams a sign? Do they mean that my wife lives?"

The priest answered comfortingly. "It is not impossible. You know that we searched the whole area. But as we found nothing to prove Luisa dead, there is, perhaps, a small chance that she survived. If so, she would surely follow us. She knew our route."

Pedro's eyes brightened. "*Es verdád!* What you say is true. If Luisa lives she will follow. Perhaps the small chance will grow into certainty and I will see her coming and hear her calling, 'Pedro, here I am, my husband.'"

In the morning, examination of the river proved discouraging. The water was high on the banks and the current rolled strongly downstream. The bottom was known to be treacherous, with shifting quicksand that would suck a team and cart down out of sight in a matter of minutes.

Antonio rode up river and then down, looking for a crossing. When he returned, he told them, "There are two camps above us. I talked with them. They warned that the river bed is dangerous. There is quicksand that shifts with a current so that it is never long in the same place. The best thought is to ride back and forth to discover rocks and potholes that could upset the carts and the soft places of quicksand."

The priest nodded, thoughtfully. "But even if you find a possible ford, look at the river. It is deep. The carts may be washed down in the current."

Antonio smiled, "These men also tell me how to float the carts across. Juan Jose, you are good with the axe. Cut lengths of those dead cottonwood logs and fasten them to the carts. This will also keep the carts out of the holes and soft spots. Tirso, you and Ramon get horses. You can help me find a ford."

It took two days of hard work but the crossing was accomplished and none too soon. The following morning, Tirso shouted from the riverbank.

"*Mira*, Padre! The river rises in the night. It is good that we are now safely across, no?"

The others popped out and rushed down to the bank.

"There must have been a heavy rain on the upper river," Antonio surmised. "It will recede later but I, too, am happy that we are across. We could have been delayed, perhaps days."

Slow progress brought them to the mouth of the pass between the mountains that rose steep on either side. Past brown fields and vineyards already cut back and mounded against the coming winter. The little settlement of Paso del Norte nestled under a haze of smoke from piles of burning leaves and cuttings.

They made camp, a cool breeze from the pass whisking the dust into little whorls and rustling the dry leaves on the ground. The priest was well aware of the longing eyes cast across the river at the lights of Paso. Over the evening meal, he cautioned again that contact with the people of Paso might lead to disaster. An incautious word, the purpose of their journey discovered, could alert the authorities and imprisonment, even death, would inevitably follow.

Lucíta listened with the others but, when the women gathered at the river to clean the supper pots, she grumbled.

"We have walked and pushed and driven ourselves across the miles from Chihuahua. Now we have a chance for a little fun and dancing. God did not put us on earth for work alone." She banged the pot up and down in the water vigorously. "Listen to the music over there. What harm to go across for an hour? Does the Father think we are stupid? That we will shout out to all that we know where there is gold?"

Rosa, her mother, snorted. "The Padre knows," she said grimly. "Where one sheep goes, the others follow. And there are some here who need only one bottle of mescal and their tongues wag freely at both ends."

The women exchanged glances and nodded agreement.

"Better for no one to cross," Elena said quickly. "To avoid trouble is easier than to mend the results." She looked to where Ramon and Fernandez were laughing by the fire.

"Keep an eye on your son, Elena," Juana joked slyly. "I'll wager he is anxious to try the fleshpots of the *cantiñas*."

"And it is your man who tempts him," Elena retorted, her eyes returning to the two by the fire. "Watch him, Juana, or you will awake in a cold bed to find Fernandez gone. It is well known that Paso wine is his favorite."

Lucíta said no more but her eyes were on Ramon. *Pues,* there was one who, like herself, liked spice and excitement. A pox on the Padre. No harm could come of a small visit, a little dancing to the tantalizing music whose sound came across the water, making her blood jump to its beat. It would be easy to slip out and back with no one the wiser.

The camp took long to settle that night. Above the gurgle of the water, the lights and noises of Paso came to them. Most were resigned to the wisdom of the Padre's admonitions. A few were resentful. The journey had been long and hard. To listen to the sounds of merrymaking so close, so inviting, irked them. The padre was well aware of their restlessness. By design he sat by the fire, watching the slow climb of the moon. Not until quiet descended and he was sure that everyone slept, did he turn to his blankets.

Elena, knowing her son's impulsive inclination, had watched Lucíta and the boy when they sauntered to the bank of the river and talked for awhile before returning to crawl into their beds. Her sleep was fitful and she rose from time to time, each time relieved to find Ramon sleeping. The moon was high when she woke again and looked at her son's tumbled blankets. Instantly, she saw that he was missing and she rushed to wake her husband.

"Andres! Andres!" She shook his shoulder. "Wake up! Ramon is gone and that witch of a Lucíta is gone also!"

Andres sat up slowly. Drowsily he squinted at his wife through sleep-fogged eyes.

"So Ramon is not in his bed. Perhaps the call of nature took him into the trees."

"No, no, Andres." Elena was distraught. "I tell you the girl is gone too. She was grumbling after the meal tonight, saying that there was no harm in a little fun and wanting to cross the ford into town. I had my suspicions when I saw her and Ramon with their heads together. Now they are gone, slipped away. You must go after them."

Andres was pulling on his boots as he listened.

"Quiet, Elena. Lower your voice. Do not wake the camp. I will speak to the Padre and if he thinks best, I will go and look for them."

Together they wakened the priest and he listened with a frown.

"Do not take this so hard, Elena," he said. "Youth likes to kick up its heels and if it is only the two who are missing, I do not think any great harm has been done. However let us check, quietly, to see if any of the others are gone. Perhaps it would be better if you go and bring them back. But not alone. I will wake Antonio while you count the ones in camp."

Only the two were missing and Lucero and Antonio saddled two horses and rode to the ford, while Elena strained her eyes into the dark after them.

Seven Was the Padre's Number 77

"I tell you, Padre, I shall have something to say to those miscreants when they return. That Lucíta is no good and Rosa has never done anything to curb her wild ways. She will destroy us. Too bad she does not have a father to take her in hand. Rosa is too easy with her."

A burst of shots came from the town and the woman clutched the priest's arm in alarm. "Oh Mother of God, protect them. What is happening? Do you think someone is shooting at them?"

The priest tried to calm her but mounting fear raised her voice and the others in camp were wakening. By the time the priest had explained the situation, they heard voices and the splashing of horses on the ford. Four riders came out of the darkness, Antonio and Lucero leading, Lucíta and Ramon following. Before anyone could speak the priest raised his voice.

"All of you get back to camp. Then we will find out what has been going on."

Fresh wood on the fire blazed up smartly and lighted the sheepish faces of the culprits.

"Now, Ramon," the priest said sternly, "let us hear about this. What have you to say?"

Ramon tossed his black hair out of his eyes. "*Diós*," he said sullenly. "What is all the fuss? So I bought a little wine for Lucíta and we danced to the music. Is that so bad?"

His father's face darkened at the insolent tone and he took the boy's arm in a grip that made him wince. "Ramon, you are too old to be whipped but I swear if you disobey orders again, I will have the hide off your bones."

The priest nodded agreement. "You both knew that to cross the river into Paso was forbidden. And you knew why. Do you think this expedition is a jaunt for pleasure? I assure you that it is serious business. Do not make me regret that I gave you permission to come with us."

Lucíta slipped close to her mother. She had pulled a corner of her *rebóso* across so that it hid all but her eyes, large with defiant apprehension. Rosa snatched her hand and pulled the girl after her toward their blankets.

"Lucíta why did you do this thing? How can you be so

selfish and willful? You would ruin us for your own pleasure."

The girl jerked her hand away and flounced down on her bed. "A lot you care about me. All you say is, 'Lucíta, the washing. Lucíta, grind the corn. Lucíta, more wood for the fire.' You never want me to have any fun. What harm did we do? Only a little while and we were already on our way back when Señor Lucero met us."

Elena's voice was shrill and the others moved closer.

"We heard shots. What was all that?"

"I do not know. We had reached the ford when we heard someone shouting and then shots," Lucíta answered sullenly.

Ramon concurred. "It was none of our doing. We had left. Perhaps a fight in a *cantiña*."

The priest sighed with relief. "It would seem that no harm has come from this escapade. But let us have no more of these tricks. I think it would be best if we move on in the morning."

"*Sí*, Padre," Antonio agreed. "It is evident that it is unsafe to camp near a settlement." His eyes scorched Ramon and Lucíta.

The camp finally settled into quiet until Antonio's shout brought them awake as the sky lightened with the coming of day. Then belongings and equipment were loaded, the oxen hitched and the little caravan moved out along the river, once more heading north. Ramon was subdued under the grim eye of his father and tried to keep as far away as possible from his mother's scolding tongue. Lucíta, moving obediently to help her mother, tried to catch his eye but he ignored her. She knew he was smarting under the disapproval of the others. Hurt pride was in every line of his stiffly held back.

Shrugging her shoulders, the girl dropped back to walk beside Tirso. Glancing sidelong at him she murmured, "Well, what are you thinking? Are you, too, ashamed of me?"

Tirso looked at her downcast face and felt his impatience with her ebbing. Wild and insubordinate she might be but there was no real harm in her. How could anyone so pretty be bad? Lucíta was only impulsive and full of life. He smiled at her.

"*Pués*, Lucíta, there was no shame in what you did. It was the fault of Ramon. He should have known better than to disobey the Father's wishes."

"Not all the fault was his," Lucíta said honestly. "I was the one to suggest going." She dropped her eyes, then raised them to his. "I have told the Padre that I am sorry and will not do anything so foolish again."

"Then let us forget it. Is it not good to have our road lie along the great river in the shade of fat cottonwoods?" He broke off, seeing that one of the carts had sunk its wheels again in soft sand. "*Carámba!*" he hurried forward to put his shoulder to a wheel with the others.

The country on either side of the river was flat and open. The Rio Bravo had flooded and scoured out a wide valley. It changed its course with each spring freshet and the floor of the valley was made up of the silt and sand carried down its winding length from the north. Cottonwoods, tamarisks, willows, and alders grew thickly with scrub filled draws cutting down to the river from the rim of the hills.

The colony kept anxious watch on these hills as they progressed. This was Indian country, peopled with the savage Apaches on the west and the dreaded Comanches on the east. They had heard the stories of the swift-moving bands that rode down to wreak their terrible vengeance on travelers, then vanishing back into the deserts and mountains out of reach of punitive expeditions sent against them.

Steadily they went north. The broad valley narrowed between encroaching hills cut by many draws hard for the carts to negotiate. Sometimes the trail left the river but not so far that the stock could not be driven down to the water.

On the fourth day out of Paso, they saw a smudge of dust on the horizon ahead, too large for a rider. Their first alarm quieted as they saw that its slow approach indicated another caravan rather than Indians. All day they watched the dust cloud and, as it neared, saw the shape of four *carrétas* emerge. The sun was lowering when they met. Canvas stretched between poles on the carts formed shade for the women and children who huddled in them. The men of the party rode alongside, each armed with muskets and sidearms. Antonio and the priest rode to meet them and the carts ground to a halt. Bone tired, their dust-caked faces showing marks of the weary days behind them, the men did not offer to dismount.

"*Hóla, compádres.*" Antonio greeted them. "You have traveled far. Can you tell us of the road north?"

One of the men who seemed to be the leader hawked the dust from his throat, spat, and spoke. "It is a road, *amigos*. That is all. Two days behind us is a waterless desert. Take care not to enter it without all the water you can carry. Mountains cut off the river, but with luck, two days will see you through to where the trail rejoins the valley of the Bravo. From there to Santa Fe is easier. What of the road south? Any trouble?"

"No trouble," Antonio replied. "From here to Paso del Norte is good, with no water problems. If you go south to Chihuahua, you have more desert ahead. Samalayucca and barren mesas to Laguna de Enciníllas and beyond."

The father interposed, "Señor, what of Indians? Have you had any encounters with our red tormentors?"

The leader spoke again. "I was about to tell you of that, Padre. We have seen none of the devil's spawn, only the ruin they leave behind. At mid-day yesterday we came on the burned refuse of two carts and what remained of eight persons." He shuddered.

"The *carrétas* were still smoking and the stock driven off. We feared the savages might return. As you see we have women and children with us, so we did not stop. You had better keep a sharp lookout."

"You did not stop?" The priest said quietly. "Not even to bury them?"

"No, Padre." The man was defensive. "They were dead. There was nothing we could do for them and I thought it best not to endanger our party."

The priest's face was stern. "A decent burial would have taken only a few minutes time. If the Indians were close enough to know of your presence, those minutes would have made no difference to your safety. May God forgive you, señor." He turned the mule's head and rode back to where the others waited. Antonio followed and the two parties separated.

Late the next day, they came on the tragic scene of the raid. Warned by vultures circling, rising, and settling, they halted a little distance away. The men got shovels and went to do what they could. As he saw the hacked and torn remnants of six men and two women, Tirso's stomach turned and he rushed to one side to vomit. He felt ashamed of his weakness but when he saw Ramon and even some of the older men were equally sick, he felt better. Lucíta, curious as always, followed them but when she glimpsed the slaughter, her face paled and, clapping her hands to her mouth, she ran back to the women.

The work was soon done and they pulled away, leaving the rock-covered mounds, with three black crosses from the burned pieces of the carts, standing in mute tribute to the courage of those who had died in torture beside the trail.

They had not proceeded far when three men on burros came down the road.

"Ahé! *Amigos!*" Antonio called to them. Looking at their earth-stained cotton shirts and trousers and their sandaled-feet, he knew them to be farmers. "Whence come you?"

"Without speaking, they pointed toward the river. The priest rode close and the men dragged their ragged straw *petates* from their heads. The older of the men spoke respectfully.

"Father, it is good to see a holy man in this place of tragedy."

"You know what has happened?" the priest asked.

"*Sí*. We heard the howling of the *Indios* and the sound of shots. Not many. *Los póbres* must have been overwhelmed quickly. Later there was screaming." The man shook his head.

"We could do *náda*."

"How many in your village?" the priest asked.

"No village, Padre. A few of us have built a small *ranchito* in the canyon not far from the river. Ten men, three guns, and five boys old enough to fight."

"How are you called?"

"I am Augustino. These are my sons, Luis and Felipe. We came to see if there was anything to do for the dead."

"What was needed has been done," the priest replied.

The farmer crossed himself. "It is well that these *póbres* had prayers said for their souls. Many do not have that comfort."

Antonio looked at the priest and jerked his head up the road. "Time passes, Padre. We must travel on."

One of the boys pulled at his father's sleeve and whispered

something. The man listened and said roughly, "Do not bother the Father with our problems, my son."

"What is it, boy?" the priest asked.

The boy hesitated, glanced at his father's scowl and finally said, "Good Father, there is a woman in our home who sorely needs comfort and your blessing."

"Do not concern yourself with this small affair," the older man interrupted. "It is merely a woman who wandered into our *placíta,* perhaps from a passing caravan." He tapped his head significantly. "It is a sickness of the mind."

"From whence did she come?" the priest asked.

"We have questioned her, but she only sits, staring into the hills. Sometimes she mutters a name, 'Pedro.' Once she said, '*Óro. Muy distánte. Al nórte.*'"

The eyes of Antonio and the priest met. "*Diós mío,*" the father exclaimed. "Could it be possible?"

"I think, Padre, we must have a look at this woman," Antonio said. "But let us say nothing to Pedro or the others. It would be cruel if this is not the one we look for."

Leaving Andres Lucero to lead the caravan ahead, the priest and Antonio followed the farmers. The burros minced daintily down an orroyo toward the river amid brush and rocks. It was not far till the arroyo widened and they saw small fields and several mud huts ahead. Women and children were gathered to greet Augustino, the head of the *ranchito.*

Augustino made the introductions and then pointed to a woman who sat on the doorstep of one of the huts, staring straight ahead. Thin and with her hair turned white by the shock of her experiences, they had no difficulty in recognizing Luisa.

The father spoke her name and, for a minute, he thought he caught a flicker in the blank eyes. Then he shook his head. "It will take time, perhaps much time, to erase the scars of her terror."

Antonio explained to the little huddle of people how Luisa had been of their party and how, in the wind and sand of Samalayucca, they had lost her. He said he could not understand where she had heard of gold in the north. Not from them, certainly. Perhaps from the ones who had found her. He told them that they were on their way to establish a mission for the Indians.

Seeing the appeal in the eyes of the people, the Father held a brief mass, giving his blessing to the *ranchito*. Then Antonio lifted Luisa up on Pardo, in back of the Padre and they started back.

It was almost dark when they saw the lights of the campfire. Lucíta was the first to spy them and ran out, calling to the others. "They come! I see them!" As they drew closer, she stopped and peered into the gloom. "What goes on? Two ride out and three come back. *Quién es?*"

The men drew up and she stared, incredulous, at the woman who clung to the priest. "*Mádre de Díos!* It cannot be—it isn't. It is Luisa! God has answered our prayers. Pedro! Pedro! Come quickly. Luisa is returned."

As the others came running, full of astonishment at the sight of this woman, her white hair falling like a cape over her shoulders, but undoubtedly, Luisa. Pedro came pushing forward and they made way for him till he stood beside the mule and reached up his arms.

"Luisa. Luisa, my wife," he said, his voice trembling and his eyes glowing with joy. The priest lowered her gently into his waiting embrace and Pedro carried her to the fire.

He pressed her trembling body to him and murmured her name over and over.

"Luisa, my dove. Luisa, my little wife. I thought never to see you again. But you are here and I will never let you from my sight again."

Slowly, the woman raised her face to him and looked into his eyes. "Luisa, my heart, do you not know your Pedro?" he said gently. Tears filled her eyes and poured down her face.

"Pedro," she said hesitantly. Then recognition came into her face and they wept together.

The others gathered close, laughing and talking. Questions came and Antonio answered what he could. The meal that night was gay with rejoicing. Luisa sat quietly, smiling at the familiar faces of her friends, Pedro's arm about her waist and his eyes never leaving her face.

CHAPTER EIGHT

Moving north, the trail drew farther from the river. Pushing up on their right, a chain of mountains lifted a frieze of peaks in jagged columns like huge pipes, into the great dome of the sky. The priest spoke of them to Tirso, who walked beside him, one hand on Pardo's neck.

"Those rock spires remind me of the cathedrals of *España*," he said. "They are like the pipes of a great organ, carrying music into the heavens for the glorification of God."

Tirso answered, respectfully. "*Sí*, Padre, if you say so. I have never seen such a thing. But there are many things of which you have spoken that I know nothing of. Perhaps, someday I will go to far places and see all these things for myself. With the gold we find in the soldier's mountain, it would be possible, no?"

The priest smiled down at him. "Yes. The gold would make it possible. If it is found."

Each night the travelers pulled off the trail and, while the women made camp, the men drove the stock over the hills to drink and filled the skins with water for the next day's travel. The nights grew colder. Occasionally they saw buffalo feeding on the hills above the river, who shied away from the screeching clamor of the cartwheels. Surprising antelope, they had fresh tender steaks for the evening fire.

The third day, the priest pointed ahead. Rising above the low contours of the country were the sharp outline of three peaks and, behind them, a blue smudge of mountains.

"There is the landmark. Just as *Sargénto* Rivera described it to me," he said exultantly. "Three sharp peaks, like pyramids, rising from the desert. Now we are getting close to our goal."

Steps quickened and the apathy of the dull routine of travel disappeared. All day they watched the approach, as the peaks became more distinct. This was the first time the priest had mentioned the soldier's directions.

Walking behind the slow-moving *carrétas,* Lucíta clutched at Tirso's sleeve. "*Que es ésto?* What does the Padre mean? Are we close to the treasure?" she asked.

"I do not know," Tirso replied. "The Padre has never told anyone how we are to go."

"Is that true? That no one knows? And what if something happens to him? How then would we find our way?"

"*Sí!*" Maria chimed in. "There would be nothing but the long way back, empty-handed."

They looked at each other, appalled. "Do you not trust the Padre?" Dolores said scornfully. Then they became aware that the priest was just behind them. He nodded, briskly.

"My children, you have given me a thought. This is something I have considered but have done nothing about. I think it is time to act."

That evening, he spoke to Antonio and the two walked to the top of a hill and sat down. The sunset was painting the landscape with rosy light and the priest's eyes roved about, appreciatively.

"This is a country new and strange," he said, "but I find much to like. I believe, Antonio, that God is with us."

They sat silent for a little before he continued. "When we first considered this journey, it sounded very wild and dangerous. I prayed earnestly for guidance. God has given us His guidance and more. He has protected us."

"This is true, Padre," Antonio agreed, crossing himself. "The good God has been a shield between us and any who would harm us. He led us to water in the arid lands and assisted us in the crossing of the mighty Rio Bravo, where we might easily have foundered and perhaps, drowned."

"Also," the priest concurred, "do not forget, that when we had given Luisa up for dead, He led us to her. It was a miracle, in this vast country, to find her safe. A special blessing for Pedro. But, *mi amigo,* since we cannot know what lies ahead, I believe that it would be wise to have someone besides myself know the location of the soldier's mine. And since you are the *mayor-dómo* of the party, I shall entrust you."

Pleasure covered the face of his companion and he straightened his shoulders with pride. "*Sí*, Padre. You know you can trust me," he said gruffly.

The priest looked at him gravely. "Heed my words," he said. "I want no one but yourself to know of these things. If any are questioned, they cannot tell because they do not know. It is for their protection."

Antonio nodded, his face serious, and the priest went on, pointing to the sharp peaks, rising to the north. "These are a mark. There we turn to the mountains where the sun rises."

As he spoke, he took from inside his robe a folded piece of linen. Carefully, he opened its folds and spread it on the ground between them. The rays of the setting sun glowed blood red, reflecting on the white cloth and an involuntary shiver ran over the priest. Then he shrugged it away and the two bent over the map, while he told Antonio the tragic story of the dying soldier.

"Now," he concluded, "you know all that was told to me. It is a relief to share the burden of this knowledge."

"I am honored to have your trust, Padre. Don Tomás, *también*, trusted me. To have the confidence of others is something to be proud of."

"What you say is true, Antonio. In many ways we are alike. Lone men, with no wives or families. The village and its people are my family. Their confidence and trust are very precious to me."

"Forgive me, Padre. I do not mean to blaspheme, but I think God places trust in you also. Otherwise He would not have allowed you to lead us far from the security of the Hacienda Aránda."

The priest smiled and then bent to the map again. "You see, here the peaks are marked. We turn to the east and cross the plain. This is a part of the waterless desert area called the Jornado del Muerto, of which you know. We must carry water to last till we reach a spring in the mountains. Rivera told me that he went up into the mountains by way of a deep *barránca*, washed out of the mountain side. The first time, by horseback.

The second time, on foot. I do not know if we can get the carts up by that route. As you see, at the top he descended into a round valley. Here is a spring." He placed his finger on a mark on the map. "There, a peak rises from the bottom and Rivera found his mine in that peak."

Antonio's eyes sparkled. "Then we have not much farther to go, Padre."

The next night they camped at the base of the three peaks. Rising sharply from the mesa, they were separated from a small range of mountains on the west. The day's journey was halted early and the stock was driven to the river with all the water-skins draped over their backs to be filled for the dry travel ahead. After the evening meal, the priest explained that at this point they would leave El Camino and turn to the mountain chain where the blue cliffs rose in columns toward the sky. Following his pointing finger, they saw a gap in the ragged outline of the crest.

"There lies our goal. Once through that break, according to *Sargénto* Rivera's directions, it should not be far beyond."

A sigh ran through the little assemblage about the fire. Weary of dust and wind and sand, of forcing the heavy, unwieldly *carrétas* over the leagues that lay behind, the thought of the end of the trail was very welcome. No one complained of the early start next morning. An eager bustle of activity filled the camp, as the sky turned pink with the coming dawn. By the time the sun rose over the eastern crest, turning the mesa before them to gold, they were ready to move out.

"*Un moménto,*" the Padre rode close. "Here we will divide. When we leave El Camino, the wheels will cut deeply into the loose soil, leaving a plain track, easy to read for any curious ones who follow. Therefore each cart will turn separately. Divide the stock to follow them. Their tracks will help to cover the ruts left by the wheels."

Antonio was nodding agreement. "*Sí,* Padre, it is a good thought. Let us also rope some bushes of mesquite and pull them over the tracks. The boys can attend to that."

At his signal, Fernandez pulled his oxen off the road. The men drove a few of the animals after him and the women followed. A little farther and Estevan turned the next cart. Again, some of the animals were driven behind, treading down the soil broken by the wheels. Juan Jose took the third cart into a wide turn so that now three columns, instead of one, proceeded easterly. Ramon, Tirso, and the Cruz boys, Juanito and Andres, dragged brush back and forth for a little distance to obliterate the marks of their passage.

All day they pushed across the flat tableland, cut by dry washes that impeded the progress of the carts. At dusk, Antonio brought the three parties together for a dry camp.

"Conserve the water," he ordered. "There is no water in the Jornádo del Muérto. We must reach the mountains before we will find any source of water. We will rest until the moon rises and then move on. Traveling at night we will escape the thirst that comes with the heat of the day."

Three hours passed before the moon was bright enough for travel. Cups of hot *atóle* warmed them in the cold night air. Then they started on. Dolores's eyes were dreamy.

"Look, Tirso," she said, with a sweep of her arm at the spaces around them. "Everything is silver in the moonlight. This morning we walked in golden light and tonight we walk in silver. Is it a sign of riches?"

"You notice everything, Dolores," he replied. "You see beauty in all. Do you not notice the sand and dust? Do mesquite thorns and cactus not scratch you? You only speak of the beauty around you. The rippling of the river, the sunsets and sunrises, the mountains. You are different from all other girls."

"Ah, Tirso, sobersides." Dolores took his hand and swung it as they walked. "Do you not know that to look for pleasant things makes the pain of scratches and ache of tired muscles less?"

The boy looked at her and shook his head in admiration.

The stars faded and the mountains showed blue in the distance. Then with the coming of the sun, the peaks ahead seemed to catch fire, rimming the horizon in red and gold. By noon they were climbing as the ground rose to gentle foothills. The priest kept a sharp eye on the land ahead. At last he gave a shout and rode to the front, pulling Pardo up beside a great conical boulder. As the others approached he exulted. "This is the next landmark. A little more and we should find a large *barránca* that runs up to the gap. Just as the soldier described it."

It was as he said. A short distance beyond, they came to the broad mouth of an arroya that debouched onto the mesa. Antonio pushed back his hat and looked up the winding boulder-strewn course. Chamisa and mesquite grew among the rocks and an occasional stunted cedar marked the hillsides.

"It does not look too easy for passage with the *carrétas*," he remarked. "Let us camp here. After we have eaten, this route can be examined more carefully. It may take several days."

"We can do that, Antonio," Ramon said eagerly. "Tirso and I will climb up and see what is ahead."

Tirso's eyes were bright. "*Sí*, Antonio! Soon it will be dark. Let us go now. We can soon tell if it is possible to take the *carrétas* up the *barranca*. If it is too narrow or steep, other ways can be considered *en la mañana*." The boys were almost holding their breath as they waited for his answer.

Antonio considered. "*Pués*, why not?" His broad face was sympathetic. "For us older ones, a day's work is enough, but for the young, they do not tire. It may save us time, *también*. Go then, but see that you are back by dark. I have no desire to climb into the rocks looking for you after the sun sets."

Lucíta was hopping up and down. "*Yo también*," she burst out. "I too wish to go."

"No, Lucíta," her mother vetoed quickly, frowning. "What are you thinking of? Going off with two boys. It is out of the question."

"Oh, Mama!" Lucíta was impatient. "You have an evil mind. Dolores will come." She whirled on the other girl. "You want to come with us, no? After all, Dolores, who knows what we may find? Perhaps we will be the first to see the *soldádo's* gold."

The priest smiled, shaking his head. "No, children. The mine is not in the canyon. We merely wish to find out if oxen and carts can get up. Then we proceed from there."

Antonio spoke sternly. "Keep in mind that you are not exploring for the mine, but to look for passage. And do not stop to pick flowers. The sun is two hours high and I want you here, on this spot, by sundown. Otherwise—," he frowned fiercely.

"*Sí, sí!*" Ramon and Tirso were already moving before any objections could arise and Lucíta and Dolores scrambled after them. The others fell to setting up camp for the night.

It was full dark, the meal had been cleared away and Rosa and Elena casting anxious glances up the canyon when the four returned. Rosa's sharp eyes went over her daughter, speculatively. Then apparently satisfied with what she saw, she turned back to the fire.

At a motion from Antonio, the two boys joined him at the fire. Every one sat up to listen.

"And what did you find?" he asked.

Ramon answered first. "As you have seen, the mouth of the *barránca* is broad, with a sandy bottom. Beyond the bend, farther up, it narrows and deepens but it is wide enough for our use."

"*Sí*, it is wide enough," Tirso added, "but in places it is very steep," he tilted his hand to indicate a steep slope. "I do not think the carts can be pulled up."

Antonio looked at the priest and shook his head. "Perhaps in the morning another and easier way can be found."

"We can try," the priest said. "I believe we can find a way. God has been with us all the long days of travel. It requires faith, Antonio, and some effort, of course."

The next few days were spent in a search of the terrain but no easier route was found. Finally, it was decided to attempt the canyon. Sprawled about the fire the tired men discussed the difficult places in the ascent. The lower canyon had no problems but in the upper levels, the rock walls narrowed and in places it was so steep that it was doubtful if the carts would pass.

"Then let us take the *carrétas* apart and carry them up," Juan Jose said easily.

"I remember the time Don Tomás ordered the great chest from the woodcarvers of Zacatécas." He slapped his knee. "We were delayed in returning because those indolent *peóns* had not finished the work on the chest. While we waited, a storm occurred which ruined the road. *Cuérpo de Christo!* You would not believe the hardships of that journey. Uncounted times we unloaded that accursed chest. In places, my friends, we repaired the road and three times, *mi compádres,* we dismantled the *carréta* and carried it and the cursedly heavy chest through ravines cut by the storm water." He glanced around at the faces turned toward him.

"So, Juan Jose, what happened?" asked Rosa, knowing the answer for she had heard the story many times.

"What happened? Don Tomás had placed his confidence in me, the best driver in all Mexico. And, my good woman, he was not disappointed. I brought the chest, as promised, and with hardly a scratch."

"That is not what the Señóra said," Rosa retorted. "Dolores rubbed the skin from her fingers, removing the marks of the journey."

Juan Jose snorted but before he could speak, the priest interrupted. "That is the solution, *hómbres.* We will unload and carry everything up the *barránca.* Then the stock can be driven up and lastly, attention will be turned to the carts. I am not willing to leave them behind to point the direction of our going. Therefore we will carry the parts up piece by piece."

The men groaned at the thought of transporting the heavy wheels but Antonio spoke with decision. "It is the best way. In fact the only way. Let us turn into our blankets. We will have a hard day tomorrow."

The foreman woke the camp at gray dawn and by the time the sun was stretching fingers of light to probe the darkness of the canyon, the line of the colony was moving slowly up the winding ascent, each with a load. Antonio led and the priest brought up the rear. Following the bends in the canyon, they soon lost sight of the camp below. As they climbed toward the top, the canyon deepened and rough, rock walls hemmed them in. The rushing torrents of decades of storms had cut deeply down from the crest, tearing out this ravine, but leaving ledges of rock that gave them a precarious footing. About halfway up, a ledge widened and Antonio called a halt to rest. Estevan leaned back on his pack and blew a long breath.

"This is not an easy way to bring up the *carrétas,* Padre. And when we reach the top after all this labor, what then? Do we go down again?"

The priest spoke slowly. "We have followed the directions laid out by *Sargénto* Rivera before his death and when we reach the top, you will see the end of the trail that he described to me."

Weariness was wiped from the faces turned to him. Eager anticipation filled them with the news that their goal, which had drawn them so far, was at last so near. A gabble of excited speculation broke out, each anxious to know more. However, the priest would not add anything, saying they would see for themselves.

Antonio nodded approval. The priest had given them the incentive to go on up the difficult trail, the steepest part of which lay ahead. They climbed with a will, over rocks and debris left by storm tossed waters and at last, reached the top. They gathered on the rim, looking down into a huge bowl, three or four miles across and hundreds of feet deep, sunk in a circle of the mountain peaks. Greasewood and cactus grew on the slopes, with an occasional stunted cedar. In the bottom a lone peak rose and at its foot cottonwoods and tamarisks indicated the presence of a spring. Not a sound broke the quiet of the great basin and, suddenly, Rosa shivered.

"Padre, what is it? What is it about this place that chills me?"

The others felt it too. Although the sun was hot on their backs, wet with sweat from the climb, a cold air seemed to rise from the deep valley before them. Then Antonio shook his shoulders, as if shrugging away a bad dream.

"What foolishness is in your minds. Are we children to be frightened of nothing? Down there lies our riches. Let us go down and see if we have been following a *chiséra,* a spirit of the mountains. Or if Rivera's words were true."

His voice broke the spell and they followed him down the slope, talking, at first softly, then as they gained confidence, shouting and laughing. The padre followed more slowly. The premonition of evil was strong, like invisible eyes watching him. He closed his hand over the crucifix that hung from his neck and tried to put his misgivings aside. The sight of his people laughing about the gurgling spring under the trees restored his faith that God had directed them here and he strode forward with confident step to join them.

CHAPTER NINE

The weary colony camped that night among the trees, near the spring that bubbled from under an outcropping of rock. The great peak towered over them and they lifted their eyes to it, speculating aloud on the gold that lay hidden somewhere in its somber depths. When they had eaten the priest led them in a simple ceremony and prayer of gratitude to the Lord for bringing them safely through the long and tedious journey and asking for His continued guidance and protection. Later, stretched in their blankets about the dying fire, the shadows of night deepened and a lopsided moon arose, casting a pale light over the great basin. Tall yuccas showed black in its light, like the feathered warbonnets of Indians. Long shadows twisted in grotesque patterns formed by the brush and cactus swaying in the light wind that rustled through the rocks.

To the priest there was a sinister quality in the moonlight. The deep valley was beautiful in the silver and black of the night but he could not shake off the disquiet that filled him. A feeling as if there were eyes watching, something waiting in the shadows. Unable to sleep, he rose and walked back up the trail to the rim. Here he remained for some hours. In the shimmer of the moonlight, the basin appeared like a sunken lake and, on the other hand, the canyon dropped blackly below the cliffs to the silvery mesas, stretching away to the distant river. To the south, the mountains of the organ pipes lifted into the sky. Doubts of his own wisdom and lack of confidence in his ability crowded into his mind. Yet, what could he do except to go on?

There was no alternative. In a few weeks they would know if this expedition would lead to success or failure. In the meantime, work and pray and trust in God's wisdom and love.

The moon was setting when he went back down to his bed. Looking about at his sleeping companions about the dead ashes of the fire, he groaned a little under the sense of responsibility for their well being.

The week that followed was one of heavy labor. Back and forth they toiled bringing up the supplies from the mesa. The stock was led up and turned loose to graze on the grass that grew thickly on the floor of the basin. Then began the dismantling of the *carrétas*. Piece by piece they were hauled up the difficult trail. Last of all, the heavy wheels were roped and dragged up, one by one.

Their efforts proceeded with only minor incidents until the last of the great wheels was being brought up. The big black ox, Samson, with Juan Jose at his head, had been pulling the ponderous wheels all day. Now he decided it was time to rest. They had reached a place where the ledge narrowed, with Antonio and Lucero guiding the unwieldy wheel, scraping over the rocks. Samson slowed and came to a halt. The big splayed hoofs stepped back to a comfortable hollow. The rope slackened and the wheel turned slowly back, toppling to lean against the cliff wall. Antonio's hands were torn loose from their grip. There was a shriek from Lucero as the wheel settled back, pinning the unlucky man's legs.

Juan Jose pulled and tugged at Samson, yelling commands, *"Arre, buéy! Andale! Andale!"* Samson grunted as Juan Jose whacked him with his pole and at last moved on, freeing Lucero's legs. He was only partly conscious as Antonio bent over him and there was blood on his trousers.

"Lie still, *amigo*. I will be back for you." Antonio leaped ahead to steady the wheel. Samson moved steadily upward to the rim and others took over. Antonio and Juan Jose ran back to the injured Lucero, conscious now and sitting up to rub his numbed legs. It was Juan Jose who lifted him, gently, and carried him to the top, his broad back dark with sweat.

A blanket was brought from the camp and Lucero was carried down. Ramon ran toward them with Elena close behind. Both were pale with anxiety and Elena was crying. "Andres! Andres! What have you done? They said a wheel fell on you."

"It is nothing very bad, *querida*. The wheel fell against me with not too much damage, I hope. I feel nothing, so it cannot be too bad."

"Mother of God, help us." Elena pressed a hand against her pale lips.

The father was waiting when the little cortege arrived at the camp. He knew only that the wheel had struck Andres and he bent over the injured man in dread of what he might find.

"It is my legs, Padre," Andres told him reassuringly. "Only my legs. At first I felt nothing but now the pain strikes." His face twisted and his teeth clenched.

"Hand me your knife, Ramon," the priest said to the boy, who had fallen to his knees beside his father. "I must slit his trousers."

Ramon, his face the color of putty, fumbled clumsily at his pocket, his eyes on his father. It was Tirso who pressed a knife into the priest's hand and helped him get the boots off. When the legs were laid bare, bloody and bruised, Elena covered her eyes and the other women broke into wailing. The priest moved his hands gently up and down Lucero's legs, his face grave in concentration, touching the bones. Then he sat back on his heels, shaking his head.

"I do not know how this can be," he said. "It is a miracle. The wheel must have been deflected. I can find no break in the bones, only bruising. It may be that the bones are cracked but if Andres lies still, they will mend. We must watch for infection. Dolores, bring me the brandy in my pack. He will need it. Elena, get hot water and clean him. Wash away all this dirt and blood."

His rapid fire of orders sent the women scattering to bring cloths, basins of water, and corn meal for poultices. Antonio went to contrive splints and the others got busy skinning and cutting up a small deer that Beltrán Cruz had shot that morning. Turning, the priest caught sight of Ramon's stricken face and patted his shoulder, sympathetically.

"Come, my son, you can help too. Go and find some vines of *toláche* or moon lily. Bring me the blossoms and roots. This injury is going to be very painful and the ground roots and flowers will lessen the pain and let him sleep. Seeds from the burrs will also be useful for the poultices." Ramon jumped up, grateful for action. Tirso joined him and they raced away to search the gullies and arroyos for the plants.

The priest looked over his people with deep contentment. Blue twilight was falling in the basin. The supper fires glowed cheerfully. The smell of roasting venison pervaded the air as the women bustled about, calling to each other happily. Lucero lay outstretched on a pad of blankets, his injured legs packed and splinted, his eyes closed. The father smiled. Such children, he thought. So dependent. Capable, confident, and able in the daily routine of life but under pressure, helpless, unsure, unable to make a decision. They needed someone to turn to, to trust. He shook his head and, turning, his eyes met Antonio's and they exchanged smiles of understanding.

When they had established themselves in the basin, the men turned eagerly to the task of finding the mine that the soldier had covered and left. The father referred to his map and pointed out the area to be searched. With loud whoops and laughter, the men turned to it. The women watched them go with cries of encouragement and then chattered happily as they went about their work. All but one. Lucíta, glancing slyly about, waited till her mother turned her back and then slipped away towards the slope of the peak where the men had disappeared. Gathering up her skirts she scrambled up among the rocks and brush like a goat.

The men were spread out through the rocks, half hidden by the chaparral and cactus growth. A light wind was rising whipping the girl's skirts against the spikes of the yuccas and the thorny branches of the mesquite. Spying Tirso ahead, she called to him peremptorily. "Wait for me! Hold up, Tirso!"

He turned, surprised. "Lucíta! I might have known. You

Seven Was the Padre's Number

were never one to stay behind and wait for news." He held out a hand to help her as she scrambled up, sending rocks clattering down the slope.

"Whoo," she panted. "It is very steep. Have you found nothing? Not even a trail?"

"*Nada*. No signs of anything. We are spread out like dogs on a rabbit trail. If we find anything, we are to shout."

Back and forth, they worked, zigzagging across the slope, searching the outcroppings and looking into the clumps of brush. Occasionally they saw one of the others. Then Lucíta glimpsed Ramon and turned quickly to call to him. Her shoes slipped on the hard gravel and shot from under her. Over and over she tumbled, rolling down the mountain side, clutching at the brush that slipped through her fingers, until she landed with a jolt against a stunted cedar in a clump of mesquite. For a moment she lay there, collecting her wits. She heard Tirso's voice as he bent over her.

"Lucíta! Are you hurt? *Un moménto* and I will have you up."

He took her hands and pulled her, swaying, to her feet.

"That was a hard fall. Are you all right?" he asked.

Brushing dust and dry leaves from her skirt, she turned up the hem and bent to examine her knee which smarted painfully.

"Just a little skin. Nothing serious," she said, laughing a little shakily.

"You have some nasty scratches," Tirso said. "The thorns of the mesquite are cruel."

"Nothing to bring those thunderclouds to your face," she replied. Then, looking at the spot where she had landed, she clutched at his hand and pointed. "*Mira! Mira*, Tirso. Look! There is a big hole under the bushes."

With rising excitement, the two pulled at the bushes to expose a tunnel that seemed to lead back into the mountain. Tirso leaped to the top of a boulder and shouted, waving to the others to attract their attention.

"*Hola! Hola!* We have something here. Come quickly and see."

The men soon gathered at the entrance, peering into its depths and exclaiming in wonder and triumph.

"*María Santíssima!* This is the place. Lucky ones. How did you find it?" Antonio's voice was husky with excitement.

"Lucíta fell into it," Tirso chuckled, his eyes twinkling.

The girl glared at him. "So you think it is funny that I fall. Perhaps you do not mind that I almost break my neck, finding your mine for you."

Ramon pushed through to examine the square entrance in the rock. "*Que páso?* Why do we stand here? *Vámanos, amigos.* Let us see what is inside."

Antonio laughed. "Not unless you are a cat that can see in the dark. We will make torches. Let us go down to the camp and tell them the news."

Lucíta gave a little shriek and whirled about to start down the peak. "I will be the first to tell. I found it." Her coppery hair blazed like a torch in the sun as she sped ahead. The women stopped their work and gathered to watch her plunge toward them. Questions poured out as she stopped.

"What is it?"

"Not another accident?"

"Who is hurt?"

Lucíta shook the hair out of her eyes. "No one is hurt. I found the mine, at least the opening in the mountain looks like it, Antonio says. Now the gold will pour out and fill our bags. We are rich." She threw her head back and laughed and the women laughed with her.

"Is it true?" they called to the men who straggled down to join them.

The priest came forward from where he had been helping build shelters of brush, plastered with mud. His sleeves were rolled back and his robe pinned up. His bared arms and legs were covered with wet clay and his face was streaked with the sticky mud.

"Is it true?" he echoed. "Have you found the mine, Antonio?"

"It would seem so, Padre. There is the entrance to an opening and from the marks of tools, it is without doubt dug by man, not animals."

"It must be," the priest cried. "Surely there cannot be two mines dug in this place."

"We will make torches and go in," Antonio replied. "Then we will know."

Joyful excitement reigned. Gay voices chattering and singing. Juan Jose and Ramon produced their guitars and some whirled around in giddy dances. Lucíta held the center of attention as the women exclaimed over her scratches. The priest beamed on his mercurial children.

Examination of the tunnel by the flickering light of the torches showed a lengthy passage, rather narrow and barely high enough to stand in. It went back about fifty or sixty feet in the rock and ended in a pile of broken stone.

"What is this?" Juan Jose exclaimed, staring at it.

"A cave-in?"

"No, no, *amigo*," Estevan said slowly. "See. The roof and wall are solid. This rock did not fall."

"Bring up some sacks and shovels," Antonio said. "We must clear out here and see what goes on."

Leather sacks were filled, passed out, dumped, and brought back to be refilled. As the pile of rubble decreased, eyes widened as a core of white quartz showed in the end of the tunnel. Antonio, with a stroke of the shovel, raked the rock away and a shout went up. Glittering in the light of the torches, the quartz was streaked and clotted with gold.

Cries of *"Oro! Oro!"* and a babble of voices echoed down the tunnel to the others. Cleaning out the rest of the rubble, Estevan broke out a huge chunk of the quartz and it was carried out to the entrance to be marveled over.

"Ah, this is beautiful," Elena said in an awed voice.

"Look at it shine," Lucíta's voice for once was soft, as she stroked the rock reverently.

"This is what we came for," Ramon pounded Tirso on the shoulder.

"It fills the eye," Tirso answered.

Dolores slipped her hand into his. "How glad I am that we

have really found the soldier's gold. Many times, I wondered if it was only a dream."

"*Sí*," Luisa agreed. "How wonderful it will be to fill our sacks and return to the hacienda. What joy we will bring."

"How long will it take, Padre?" asked Ramon. "How long before the ore sacks are filled?"

"Many days of hard digging," the priest told him with a wry smile.

Andres Lucero laughed, shortly. He sat, his injured legs spread stiffly out in front of him, with his back against a boulder. Antonio had cut splints that immobilized them but they still gave Lucero a good deal of discomfort.

"You speak truth, Padre," he said. "It is very hard work, as some of you know having worked in the mines of Aquíles Serdán. This piece the men brought down looks very good. But who knows if the vein will continue. Perhaps it will pinch out. Is this not so, Beltran?" he appealed.

Beltran Cruz, carrying an iron bar and mallet, stopped to smile at them.

"Hard work and slow," he answered. "*Pico y pála*, pick and shovel and these," he shook the mallet and bar. "It is the nature of gold to be difficult and much rock must be broken to get it out."

"What are those for?" Ramon asked, his eyes bright with curiosity.

"To make holes for the black powder to break out the wall rock," Beltran replied. He went on, "Andres *y* Juanito, do not stand here spending the gold we do not yet have. *Ándale niños!* Help Pedro bring stones to build a pit by the stream to wash out the gold."

"Pedro can use help," the priest agreed. "Tirso, you and Ramon brag about your muscles. Let us see proof."

Turning to Lucero, he went on, "*Cómo le vá*, Andres? Do your legs pain you very much?"

"They are not good, Padre. I can tell you that."

"The accident was a bad thing. But you are fortunate that it was no worse. It will be several weeks before you can stand but Estevan will carve you some crutches and after the swelling is gone perhaps you can get around on them. It will be less tiresome."

"You are right, Padre. My legs could have been crushed beyond repair. I have thought of the cripples that sit in the plaza at Chihuahua."

"Do not worry, Andres. You will not be a cripple. Have faith in the Lord and patience to await His healing."

The work was soon organized. Pedro cut and fitted the stones that the boys brought and piled by the stream. A stonemason and an artisan, every stone was cunningly cut and fitted so perfectly that the walls of the pit would hold water like a cup. Only a little caliche mixed with water was necessary between the tight joints of stone. The priest nodded his head approvingly.

"Good work, Pedro."

Pedro looked up and swept off his hat. A red cotton cloth was tied about his head to keep the sweat from running into his eyes. "Hot work, Padre, and hard, but it is a step. A step toward our dream, when we fill our carts with gold and go back to the hacienda. It will be a good tank that will hold the water to wash this gold." He returned to his work.

The father turned to look up at the peak, where the men toiled up and down from the mine. Antonio had the work going smoothly. As the gold-laden quartz was brought down, it was dumped on a huge flat-topped rock and broken up to free the shining metal. So large was the vein that good-sized pieces were recovered. When Pedro's tank was finished, the women would wash the dust and particles out.

As the days went by, the tunnel lengthened, winding deeper into the mountain, following the vein. Winter deepened and nights were bitter cold, although the days were sun-warmed and pleasant. Brush lean-tos had been built and plastered with mud to give some protection against the cold.

Then, one day, a blast opened a hole in the end wall of the tunnel. The astonished men peered through the opening into a dark cavern. The muted roar of rushing water came to their ears and a torch thrust into the darkness revealed a huge cave. The word went quickly down to the camp and the people gathered at the entrance, apprehension darkening their faces.

Estevan came out to talk to them, a worried frown on his face. "This may be the end of our gold mine, Padre. We have broken through into a great cavern, hollowed out by an underground stream. It may be that the river has washed away the vein."

"God's will, *amigos*," the priest said, quietly. "If it is gone, it is gone. But let us explore the cavern. Who knows, we may find the river has merely cut the vein."

Beltran shook his head discouraged. "It is not likely. Once lost, a vein is not easy to relocate. But, as you say, we will look."

The window in the tunnel was enlarged and more torches brought. One by one the men followed Estevan into the dark unknown. Once inside, the torches revealed a huge cave scoured out of the rock by the underground river that growled along the floor, emerging from the dark reaches beyond the light of the torches and disappearing into a yawning crevice at the end of the great cavern. Amazement and awe held them almost speechless.

"There is room for an entire caravan here," Antonio said in hushed wonder. "And notice! The air is fresh. The smoke from the lights rises. There must be an opening above."

Cautiously, they edged toward the river and gazed at the black, icy water rushing through. Then a muffled shout from Estevan, "*Mira! Andale! Mira al oro!*"

Following the sound of his voice, they found him in another cave. Silhouetted in the light of his torch they saw him and, beyond, a great streak of quartz surrounding a wide, glittering vein of gold. Crowding in behind him, none spoke, and they stood in silence. Then the voice of the priest broke in, reverently.

"What a revelation of God's mercy and love," he said.

"Not only the golden wealth, but a fortress to protect us from our enemies."

He had been quick to see the security which the caverns offered. Now the others realized the truth of his words and, at his signal, fell on their knees to join in a prayer, giving thanks for their blessings.

That evening the father and Antonio talked long after the

chattering and singing of the others had ceased and the camp slept.

"Who could have guessed," Antonio marveled, looking up at the dark bulk of the great peak, "that within the mountain a colossal *cavérna* exists, carved by the dark water. It is fearsome to think about."

"The work of the Lord is often fearsome and awe inspiring," the priest replied. "That He has opened this refuge to us is surely a sign of his favor."

"A rich refuge, Padre. Inside the *cavérna del Mina*, we will be warm in the cold of night."

"And enemies cannot find us," agreed the priest.

"Enemies, Padre? We do not seem to have any," Antonio said thoughtfully. "Neither *Índios* or wild animals seem to come into the basin. It is strange, I have seen deer on the other side of the rim and wolves howl on the mesas. I have seen the tracks of a big cat in the canyon by which we came but inside the valley, *náda*. It is as if the basin is *maldíta*, evil."

"Or perhaps that the Lord guards us against any evil that approaches," the priest said gravely.

They sat without speaking for a time as the silence of the night closed around them. At last, Antonio spat into the fire and said, "Padre, another thing has arisen. Rosa tells me that soon we must have corn."

"I have been aware that this would arise and I have given it thought. The little *ranchito* on the river that we passed, it is not too far."

"Padre, what is it that you fear?" Antonio looked at the priest closely.

The priest was slow in answering. "It is not the savages or the wild beasts, my friend. Even though they are bad to encounter. It is the Church."

Antonio waited for him to go on and, when he did not, said, "The Church, Padre? What do we have to fear from them? Surely they will approve of their subjects bettering themselves and the Church too."

The priest laughed a little bitterly. "No, *amigo*, I have seen it happen before. The Church will only approve of riches for themselves. If they discover where we are and what we have, they will take it and, perhaps, our lives also."

"Our lives!" Antonio exclaimed. "What good would our lives be to them?"

"If there are no tongues to tell, there are no awkward explanations to make," the priest said. "That is why I have tried to cover our trail in every possible way. I do not know how long it will take the authorities to discover that we are gone and set out to trace us. But it is possible and we must take great care not to bring ourselves to the attention of any who might assist them."

"Then we must send someone who can be trusted to keep a quiet tongue," Antonio said thoughtfully. "It comes to my mind that Lucero is the one. He is clever enough not to be followed and will keep a close mouth."

The priest frowned. "It is a long way, even to the ranchíto. Will his leg trouble him?"

"He will have to take a horse to bring back the corn so he can ride one way and, perhaps, part of the way back. His leg is much better. In my opinion he can do it."

"So be it. Lucero will go for supplies," the priest agreed. "He will have to pay for it with some of the gold. Do you think a small sack of dust will arouse too much talk?"

"He can say that he is from the north and that he got the gold there," Antonio suggested.

"Yes. That might be believed. I know it is wrong to deceive but, when the lives of all depend on it, I think the Lord will forgive. Talk to Lucero in the morning."

CHAPTER TEN

Elena Lucero's heart was heavy. She walked up the trail to the rim with Andres. Ramon, leading a saddled black and the grey mule, Pardo, was behind. Reaching the top where the canyon dropped away, they looked across the mesa to the west where a faint dark line marked the river.

The woman sighed. "It is so far, Andres. Your legs need more time to heal and to gain strength."

"I am fine, my wife. Also, I am riding, not walking. Do not worry about me."

"There were others who could go. Why did the Padre choose you?"

"The Padre and Antonio agreed that I am the best choice. I am not of much use at the mine and it would slow the work to take an able man away for this journey," Andres patted her shoulder.

Ramon spoke, wistfully. "I wish I could go with you, my father. I could be of help to you."

"I can do anything that needs to be done," Andres replied. "It is not a difficult thing to ride to the *ranchito* and buy the necessities. I will return in a few days, a week at the most. You, my son, must look after your mother. When I am away, it relieves my mind to know that you are here to care for her."

"You have water and enough to eat," Elena's eyes checked the pack on the horse. "Jerky, tortillas, and ground corn. Be careful, my husband, and return soon."

She threw her arms around his neck. "I wish you would not go, Andres. I need you, too. I have a feeling of bad luck and I would die if you did not return to me. Many things can happen out there alone on the trail."

"Hush, my wife." He put his arms around her. "I can take care of myself. The Padre has his reasons for choosing me and he is our friend as well as our leader. I will be back in a week. Do not worry. Now, I must go. The sooner I start, the sooner I will return."

He took the reins from Ramon and mounted. The boy handed him Pardo's lead rope and stepped back beside his mother. The two watched as the trail down the canyon took him out of their sight. After a bit, he reappeared at the bottom and they saw him wave before he set off across the mesa, growing smaller and smaller until only a little dust marked his progress.

Lucero's thoughts were on the conversation he had had with the priest when they had discussed the trip. He was troubled at the priest's belief that the Church would send soldiers to find and punish them. Once it was known that they had left Don Aránda's hacienda to seek gold without the permission of Church authorities, retribution would be certain, the priest warned. He had been emphatic about the danger that could ensue if the colony was traced.

Why would the Church be angry? This puzzled him. Had not the Padre written many times during the years of the drought for aid from the Church? And had his face not been sad when no word came from the Bishop in Mexico City. No word and no assistance. Why then, could the Church be angry if the people no longer needed help? He shook his head. Still, the padre had been disturbed and since he knew much more about the Church than anyone else, it must be true. And if soldiers were sent, it was a different matter. One could expect no mercy from the military. That much, he could understand. It was important, the priest had insisted, that he be as inconspicuous as possible.

He camped that night in the thick growth of trees along the river and arrived at the *ranchito* the next day. The small *placita* was serene in the warm sun. Women were grinding corn and the shouts and laughter of the children at their games filled the air. The fall work was done and the men lounged about, talking. A look about showed him the long storehouse, its open doors revealing piles of corn, squash, and pumpkins, strings of dried figs and melons, and great loops of red chili. The animals had been turned into the stubble of the stripped fields to forage for themselves before it was time to replant for the next season.

Conversation ceased and all eyes turned on the stranger as he rode up to the well in the center of the *placita*. Dismounting, he removed his hat and slapped the dust from his clothes. Approaching the group of men about the well, he spoke politely.

"*Buénas días, señóres*. A little water, *por favór,* for my animals and myself."

At their nods of acquiescence, he let the horse and Pardo move to the watering trough towards which they were already stretching their heads. A wooden bucket stood on the stone edge of the well and he dropped it, bringing it up, dripping, and taking a gourd dipper from the windlass, drank long and deep.

"Ah-h," he said, wiping his face. "Cool and sweet. *Muy*

buéno, after the long, hot road from the north."

A heavy man had come from one of the houses and now elbowed his way through the group. The others moved back to let him through.

"You are from the north, *hómbre?*" he asked.

"*Sí.*"

"You travel alone? A brave man, to ride El Camino Real without companions."

"Not brave. Of necessity." Lucero smiled.

"It is said that bandits ride the Camino. Men who rob and then kill, to leave no informants. Or Apaches, who tie their captives to ant heaps. You met none of these?"

"I have seen no bandits or *Indios*. I do not want to see them," Lucero answered. "But I have not been alone long. My wagon is with a caravan camped two days ride to the north. Three *carrétas,* five men, and our wives and children."

"What is your name and why do you come to our village?"

"Andres Castillo," Lucero answered, thinking quickly. "The reason for my visit is simple. Bad luck, *amigo.* A wheel was broken. It takes time to repair and, with this delay, our food is almost gone. So, I rode this way, hoping to find some persons who would, perhaps, sell us some corn."

"It might be arranged," the heavy man said. "Come to the fire and eat with us. Later we can talk."

"*Grácias, señor,*" Lucero said. "You make proof of hospitality. With your permission, I will care for my animals. Can someone show me where to put them?"

"Felipe. Take the mule and our friend's horse to a corral and see that they are fed," the heavy man said.

"I am Augustino Sanchez."

Lucero followed Felipe to a corral and they unsaddled Pardo and the black. Felipe brought armloads of hay and tied a thong, securing the gate. As they went back to the others, he remarked on Lucero's slight limp.

"A little injury," Lucero replied. "The accursed wheel fell against my legs when it broke. It is nothing."

After they had eaten, Augustino Sanchez sat back and looked at his guest.

"We, my family came here ten years past, come spring. Felipe was a small boy then. We have a grant for this land. Here we will stay and grow. It is good to own land and make it produce. My sons and I know the land and the noise of the corrals and the way of the crops in the fields. We also know firearms and how these lands can be protected from the savages that ride the country. How long did you stay in the north country? Have you a good reason for leaving what you gained there?"

Lucero hesitated, marshalling his thoughts. This old man was very sharp. When he answered, his voice was soft and a little sad. "Señór Sanchez, it is true. We failed in our brave attempt to make a new home. I am ashamed to say it. For three years we tried. Four times our homes were burned and some of the people were killed. In the sierras to the north, the *Índios* are bad. Very bad. Very bad. They delight in burning and raiding, stealing the women and children. The villages are never safe from them. And it is a cold land, señor. Not like this. For long months, the cold is so great that no planting can be done. You plant in May and harvest in September. Some crops do not do well in the cold. So, my uncle and his sons decided to return to Paso and I came with them."

Sanchez watched his face shrewdly. "So you are returning. After three years, do you have *pésos* to pay for these supplies which you need?"

Lucero lifted his head. "We do not come begging," he said. "We have no *pésos* but I will pay with this." He pulled a small buckskin bag from his pocket and untying the strings, he poured out a little pile of gold dust and nuggets.

Augustino Sanchez' eyes grew large. "*Óro!*" he said. "How do you come by this, *hómbre?*"

"It was gathered from the bed of a river in the northern sierras," Lucero told him.

The other men about the fire gaped and talked in low tones, awed by the sight of the gold. "Do all rivers have gold in them?" asked one. "The *paisános* must be rich, there," said another. "Why should a man labor in the fields and work with cattle, when he can gather wealth in the river?" asked another.

Lucero shook his head. "Not all rivers have gold. And there is a tax placed on what is found. If it is known."

Felipe's face was flushed and his eyes bright. "Let me hold a piece, Papa," he begged. "I have never seen gold." His father gave him a nugget and he fingered it, turning it over and over before reluctantly handing it back. "Have you more?" he asked, turning to Lucero.

"Only a little was found and divided among us," Lucero answered.

After more talk, a bargain was struck for corn and beans in trade for the gold and Lucero unrolled his blankets and lay down. The air was still and cold as he went over in his mind everything he could remember about the conversation. He must be sure that he had said nothing suspicious. Nothing that could be repeated that would lead anyone to the colony. Satisfied, at last, he rolled over and slept until the sun waked him.

It was well after noon when Pardo was finally loaded with sacks of corn, frijoles, and a little chili. Lucero remembered the salt and Sanchez hesitated but agreed to include a small amount. Salt was hard to come by, having to be gathered by salt caravans of *carrétas* lined with oxhides that traveled long distances to the salt lakes, where the salt was scooped up and brought back to be cleaned in the boiling pots by the women.

The sun was barely two hours above the western horizon when he rode out. Deliberately, he had delayed his departure, knowing that if there was any one who wished to follow, he could lose them more easily in the dark. He rode slowly at first and, then as he climbed up the curve to the highway, his pace increased. After a bit, he pulled the animals off the road and down into the thick tangle of brush and trees along the river. The shadows lengthened, as they proceeded and then dimmed as the sun dropped below the horizon. Coming to a high bank where the current had cut down heavily in floods, he dismounted and led the black down behind it, Pardo following. Here they were completely out of sight of the highway and he prepared to camp for the night. After the horse and Pardo had been watered, he tethered them close to the bank and built a tiny fire of twigs to heat water for a cup of *atóle*. Then he spread his blankets and covered the ashes of the fire. Pardo, who had been cropping grass, suddenly raised his head and turned his eyes toward the south. Lucero laid his ear to the ground and heard the beat of hooves. Someone was riding fast up the highway. He immediately got up and stood by the black horse, ready to seize his nose and prevent a whicker that would warn the rider of their presence. But the hoof beats died away in the distance and he lay down again with his gun close to his hand. A smile crossed his face and he winked at the moon, saying to himself,

"Perhaps, Felipe does not sleep tonight. It may be that he, or some other, goes to look for a caravan two days ride along El Camino."

He slept lightly, the hoot of an owl in the trees waking him once. Rising while it was still dark, he was on his way for an hour before the sun rose. Then heading east into its light, he headed for the mountains, taking care to brush out his tracks where he left the highway. The almost constant wind of the mesas would erase them completely before anyone came looking. He kept his eyes on the notch in the mountain crest and stopped only once when the sun overhead told him it was noon. Munching on cold tortillas with a wry face, he watched as the animals snatched at the tall grass and rested.

That night was another cold camp as he would not jeopardize the success of the trip by building a fire. In the morning they set out again before dawn, again resting at noon. By night they were approaching the mountains and Lucero was cheered by the thought that the next day would bring them to the canyon.

The sun was high and Elena sat on a high point of the rim, keeping close watch on the western mesa. She had been there every day, even when she knew it was too soon. Now her sharp eyes caught the glimpse of movement and a curl of dust. Dust driven before the wind had fooled her before, but now, shading her eyes against the sun, she was sure that something was moving in the little cloud wavering in the wind. In a few minutes, the shapes of the rider and a led animal emerged and her heart leaped with the knowledge of his safety. Tears of relief filled her eyes as she watched the figures grow larger until

Seven Was the Padre's Number

she saw his arm waving to her. Then she hurried down the trail to camp.

"He comes. My Andres comes." She cried. "Ramon! Go and help your father."

Ramon dropped a load of firewood and straightened. "Papa is back? *Muy buéno!* I will go to meet him. He will, without doubt, be very tired," he said eagerly.

"*Yo tambіén*," Pedro volunteered. "They are drilling in the mine and will not need me for hours, till it is time to dig out again."

"Tell your father I will have food ready for him. Just as he likes it," Elena called after them.

True enough, Elena had everything hot and ready when the men came down the trail. A skillet of venison with her own special sauce, frijoles, and hot tortillas. Pedro and Ramon tended to the unloading of Pardo and turned the animals loose to water. Elena sat very close beside her husband while he ate, smiling with pride and happy that he was returned and safe. When he finished and leaned back, wiping his mouth, he belched comfortably.

"Ah, *chiquíta*. A feast. Cold tortillas and jerky may sustain life but they are no satisfaction to an empty belly."

Now the others, who had waited politely for him to finish, crowded close to hear of his journey. The priest came up and sat down to question him.

"Well, Andres, tell us. How did it go? No trouble?"

"*Náda*, Padre. As you suggested, I told the *paisános* that we were camped two days ride north with a broken wheel and needed supplies."

"They had questions?" the priest asked.

"*Sí, sí Mádre de Diós!* Many questions. How many in our party? From where did we come? What was our destination? The condition of the trail? Had we seen Apaches?" Lucero wagged his head and spread his hands.

"And you told them—what?"

Lucero shrugged. "That we were four families from near Santa Fe, traveling together for safety to Paso. I told them we found living hard in the north and our women were homesick, so we decided to return."

"It seems believable," the priest nodded. "But did they believe? And later, when you paid them in gold?"

"Ah, that excited them." Lucero grinned. "Their eyes popped and the questions, Padre. You would have thought it was a fortune. Words poured from them. Where did we get it? And when I said that it was gathered from the bed of a river in the northern mountains, they wished to know what river. Did all the rivers carry gold? Was everyone in the north, then, rich, if gold could be picked up so easily? I tell you, Padre, the little bag of gold created much excitement."

"H'm," the priest pulled at his upper lip, frowning.

"This is not good. The people of the *ranchito* will not forget this. And probably chatter to anyone who passes."

The frown on his face deepened as he considered, then with a motion to Lucero to follow him he rose and walked away, out of hearing from the others. He questioned Lucero closely about everything that was said and done at the *ranchito*.

"Padre, I believe that one of the villages tried to follow me," Lucero said.

"As I told you, I left the road and stayed down among the trees by the river as I came north. But, after dark, I heard a horse, ridden fast, also going north on the road. I think it may have been the son of Augustino Sanchez, a sharp-eyed youth, who seemed most interested in the bag of gold."

"He did not find you?" the priest said, abruptly.

"No fear," Lucero answered. "I camped behind a high bank where the river had cut into the slope."

"Were you careful about tracks when you turned this way?"

Sí. I found hard pan and rock. Also I went back and erased all traces of passage. If the rider was Felipe, the son of Sanchez, I do not think he had enough experience to track us."

The priest was worried, nevertheless. The stir that the gold had created gave him concern and he expressed his uneasiness to Antonio that evening. The big man laid a hand on the black-robed shoulder.

"Do not let this depress you, Padre. It was a risk, but a

necessary one. The *paisános* of the river think the gold came from the far north. It should not direct attention our way."

"All very good to say," the priest retorted. "But this visit cannot be repeated. Even going to settlements farther up river will only increase suspicion if the soldiers come."

"It may not be necessary," Antonio said. "Andres brought a good supply and some can be used for planting. Then we will have our own supply."

And so it proved. The sun-warmed earth of the Basin produced the corn and beans which are the staples of life to the people. The chili plants grew and spiced the food and the seasons came and went, while the little colony labored and the hoard of gold grew.

CHAPTER ELEVEN

Dolores stood on the lip of the Basin and looked out over the wide silent land, in the glory of the fall sunset. The heat of day ebbed with the sun and the nights were turning cold. On the mountains behind her, the oak brush was beginning to redden and on the high peaks of the distant range to the east, tiny caps of white showed. A chill breeze whispered in the brush and a shiver shook her shoulders. She drew her *rebóza* closer about them. A sound on the path startled her and she whirled, relaxing as she saw the Padre close behind her.

"Ah, Dolores. I frightened you. Your thoughts must have been far away indeed if you did not hear me puffing up the slope."

The girl's eyes were large and serious, as she faced him and he realized that she was troubled. Dropping his joking manner, he asked, "What is it, *muchácha?*" He put his hand on her shoulder, "Why are you trembling?"

"I do not know, Padre. It is a feeling as if something very bad is about to happen." Her dark eyes begged him to understand. "The others, Lucíta and Elena, even Ramon, laugh at me and say it is only indigestion."

"Is that all? Only a feeling, nothing else?" the priest asked. "Is that why I have seen you often up here in the evening, looking out over the mesa?"

"*Sí*, Padre. When will we return to the haciénda? I never had this feeling there. It was always so pleasant, so safe."

"So. I understand. You are homesick, Dolores. This feeling is no more than a longing to see familiar faces again." He pinched her cheek. "Soon, *muchacha,* soon. We have labored mightily and with a will. We have torn the gold from the heart of the mountain and melted it into heavy bars of wealth. It is time to repair the *carrétas* and load them with the gold that will astonish those of Hacienda Aránda on our return."

Dolores eyes sparkled. "Oh, Padre. It will be wonderful to see them all again," she said, clasping her hands, the glow of the sunset reflected in her face.

"Come, my child. It will soon be dark and we must go down," he said, smiling at the change his words had made. He lingered a little before following her light feet, thinking of the many things to be done before they could turn their steps toward Chihuahua. He and Antonio had planned, carefully. The assembly of the carts would include reinforcing the floor, to take the weight of the gold bars. There were the crops to be gathered to supply food for the long journey back. And, finally, the complete obliteration of their camp. Everything that was not necessary for the journey would be stored in the cavern to lighten the loads in the *carrétas*. The black powder had been used sparingly. Some would be needed for the muskets on the return journey. The last of it would bring down the rock of the tunnel to cover the entrance. The last touch to preserve the rest of the treasure for the future.

The priest sighed. How he longed to be done with all of this and back in the little chapel on the hacienda. Let others have the gold. They had worked hard and suffered privation and hardship for it. For himself, he wanted only peace and a quiet spirit. Although he had said nothing to the girl, he too felt the weight of foreboding.

From the outset, his mind had been deeply troubled. It was not easy to justify the fact that he had consented, with mis-

Seven Was the Padre's Number

giving, to lead these people away from their commitment to Don Aránda and his own duty to obey the laws of Church and God. His excuse had been the betterment of the people, the hacienda, and the Church. Of late, however, doubt had been pushing into his mind. Doubt that the Church would look with favor on his defection, no matter how good the cause. Perhaps Don Aránda and the people would be happy in the fortune hidden in the *carrétas,* but again, nagging doubt crept in to darken the prospect.

He had watched the changes in his little colony, as the hoard of gold grew. It had been a close-knit, congenial little group, working and laughing together, as they had on the hacienda. Now there was less laughter and cameraderie. An air of watchfulness, almost distrust, pervaded the camp. Could this, he questioned himself, be the possession of gold creating suspicion among themselves. Surely not, since the gold was to be shared by all. It must be only that everyone was tired and anxious to return to their homes. He looked up at the sky, already darkening, with a few stars showing one by one, and prayed.

"Lord, help me. Give me the strength and wisdom to lead my people to a better way of life. Keep the demon, Satan, from filling them with unholy and evil thoughts and show them that true happiness comes only from Thy power and Thy glory."

Summer was gone. The crops that the women had planted and tended were gathered and sacked. Antonio and the priest had decided that it was time to go. Waiting only until the father came down to the fire, Antonio made the welcome announcement.

"*Oyé, compádres,* two years have passed since we left Hacienda Aránda. We have lived and worked as one. The results are satisfying. Now, it is time to go home. The black powder diminishes and must be replenished. We have more bars of gold than we can carry safely in the *carrétas.* So, we take what we can and leave the rest stacked in the cavern for another time. Tomorrow we begin the work of clearing away."

Shouts of approval greeted his words. Luisa cried out, "You hear, Pedro? At last, at last, we can go home." Tears of gladness were running down her face.

Pedro nodded, smiling. "*Sí*, Luisa. Soon we will be back with our own."

Rosa bobbed her head, emphatically, Then we can make plans for the future. It is high time Lucíta be placed in the sisters' school in Mexico City. There was never money before, but now, it is possible."

Lucíta, who had been dancing around the fire, laughing, came to a halt, frowning, her eyes turned stormy. "*Carámba*, mama! I do not wish to go to any saintly school. I am quite happy as I am."

"High time, indeed," Elena said, scornfully, "but I doubt that even the good sisters can turn this wild girl into a lady."

Rosa tossed her head. "We'll see. And you would do well to think of your Ramon. If ever a boy needed schooling and discipline, it is he."

The two women glared at each other. Lucíta giggled.

"You two look like a pair of cats on a wall," she said. "If Ramon goes to the brothers', I will wager he will teach them a thing or two. And the sisters will be glad to ship me home. Ugly uniforms and lessons and prayers, ugh! If you make me go, I will run away."

Rosa said only, "We'll see," with a glance at the father.

The priest spoke, gently. "There is much to be said for schooling. I hope to be able to bring someone to the hacienda who can teach all the children. I am sure we all have plans but let us plan wisely, for the good of all."

The long, plaintive hoot of an owl cut across the talk and silence dropped like a curtain of fear over them. Dolores' dark eyes were wide with terror.

"*Válgame, Diós*," she whispered. "This is the second night he has called."

"Three times is a warning of death," Rosa muttered, crossing herself.

Even the men sat frozen, whispering among themselves of the bad omen. The priest looked about him.

"*Amígos*, what is this all about? So an owl hunts nearby. Is he evil because he has hunger? Do not believe foolish talk about signs and evil spells. Say a few more aves tonight to cleanse your minds of such things as witches and spirits. Now everyone to bed. We have much to do tomorrow."

Bright sun dispelled the terrors of the night before and the colony set to work. Laboriously, the *carrétas* were carried back down the canyon, piece by piece, assembled and reinforced. The gold bars were brought down and carefully concealed in the bottom and covered with blankets and sacks of supplies. The great iron pots, used for melting the gold and all the tools were carried through the tunnel into the cavern. The Cruz brothers, Tirso, and Ramon demolished all signs of their life in the basin, throwing the debris into arroyos.

As they worked, Tirso had been turning over in his mind the thought of leaving the colony and heading north up the Camino del Real. The new country beckoned him as strongly as ever. Confident that he could make his own way, the thought of retracing the long weary distance to Chihuahua was distasteful. Reluctant to say anything to the padre, he nevertheless found himself following the priest on his customary walk up the trail at dusk. The father heard his steps on the rocky path and turned to wait for him. Silently, they climbed to the rim and sat down on the boulders where the trail plunged into the canyon.

Sensing that the boy had something on his mind, the priest waited for him to speak. Not knowing quite how to broach the subject, Tirso said, awkwardly, "Father, you are sad that we leave?"

"No, my son. There is always a little sadness in the ending of anything. But there is the beginning to look forward to. The beginning of the journey home and those who wait for us."

They watched the stars come out and begin their slow wheel through the sky. The boy spoke again. "This gold, Padre. It is supposed to make us all happy, *verdád?*"

The priest turned to face him. "Happiness is a relative thing. What makes one person happy is nothing to another."

Tirso considered. "True, Padre, and the gold does not mean as much to me as making my dream come true." He went on more easily, now that he had started. "You know that I have always wanted to see the north country that is being opened.

To see if the stories told by the traders of the caravans that come to Chihuahua, are true. We have come far toward the north and I would wish to go on, not back."

It was the priest's turn to consider. When he did not answer, Tirso went on. "There is nothing for me at the hacienda. Only the graves of my mother and father. Friends, but I will make new friends where I go."

"What about Dolores?" asked the priest, his eyes twinkling.

Tirso flushed a little. "I have thought, Father, but I cannot ask her to go with me until I have proved myself. Perhaps she will wait for me."

"I have no doubt about that," the priest said drily. "You have a good mind, my son, and a strong body but you are so young. I find I am reluctant to agree to let you go alone into a country you know almost nothing about. Can you not wait a little? Come with us back to the hacienda and, at Christmas, perhaps you can join one of the caravans. At least, then you will have protection to Santa Fe."

Tirso thought awhile and then said, "Padre, I have listened to your advice many times and never found it unwise. I will do as you say."

The priest patted his knee, fondly, and after a little, they started down. Lucíta's scream quickened their steps and, running in alarm, they found the people huddled close to the fire, chattering in terror. Dolores ran straight to the priest and knelt, clutching the fold of his robe to her face. The women had thrown their *rebósas* over their heads and were rocking back and forth, moaning.

Elena cried, "Padre! The owl! He came again." Andres, visibly shaken, said, "He flew right through the smoke of the fire, Padre. His eyes were glowing like red coals."

"Three times," wailed Rosa. "It is a sure sign of death."

"I said we should sprinkle salt around," Maria cried. "It might have sent the witch away. Now there is no remedy."

The priest's face flushed with anger. "Nonsense!" he thundered. "Are you *idiótas, nécios?* Sniveling children or men and women? How can you believe in the babblings and mumbo-jumbo of old wives? I tell you there are no such things or persons as witches. Now, stop all this foolishness! Ask the forgiveness of God lest you provoke his anger and destroy yourselves."

His anger did more to calm the group than any reasoning. In all the years he had ministered to their souls, they had never seen him angry. Disturbed perhaps, stern on occasion, but never angry and it shocked them to a wide-eyed, open-mouthed quiet. A heavy frown knit the priest's brow and his voice was harsh as he thrust his fingers outward and said, "Go! Go to your knees and pray that these *malinténcionádo,* godless thoughts be cleansed from you."

He drew a long breath as he watched them withdraw into the tunnel to the cavern. His anger ebbed, to be replaced by shame. Why had he lashed out at them, forgetting the teachings of God and the Church? Never, since his early years, had he so lost control. Why?

A lop-sided moon rose swiftly over the eastern edge of the Basin and grotesque, elongated shadows stretched from the rocks and cactus that encircled him. Again the heavy feeling of doom swept over him. Was it possible that the Basin was haunted by some ancient evil? No! It must be simply the restlessness of the trying years spent here, confined, away from all the familiar things of their lives. His God was all powerful. Before he slept, he prayed long and earnestly, confessing his sins of anger and impatience.

With the first early light, Antonio came stretching and yawning to start the fire. He viewed the cold ashes and spat into them. Then a shout turned him to look up at the rim where Pedro had spent the night. It had been Father La Rue's suggestion that a sentry over the loaded carts below might be wise. Seeing Pedro beckoning, he climbed to his side and followed the line of his pointing finger. A rider was coming fast, pounding over the mesa. They waited, watching, while he reached the mouth of the canyon and, with no hesitation, plunged into it.

"So," Antonio muttered, "This man, whoever he is, knows where to find us."

"*Sí,*" Pedro agreed, "how can this be? It is *muy misterióso.*"

Soon the sound of the horse's scrambling feet grew louder and then, suddenly, the pair emerged. Puzzled and more than a little disturbed, the two men stared at the youth, who promptly flung himself from the saddle and stood, frozen, staring back at them. The horse, sweating heavily from his run, stood, his legs wide apart and his breath coming in gasps.

"Who comes, *hómbre*?" Pedro challenged.

When the youth did not answer, Antonio spoke harshly. "Speak, man! Who are you? What is your purpose here?"

The boy still did not answer and Antonio turned to Pedro. "Let us take this stranger down to the Padre. Perhaps he can get some answers from him. Bring the horse." He took the rider's arm firmly, and escorted him down to the camp, where the people were beginning to move about the business of breakfast.

Confronting the priest, the boy's paralysis broke. He fell to his knees and clung to the dark robe, words pouring out in a confused babble, quite unintelligible. The priest laid his hands on the trembling shoulders and waited for him to control himself. The others crowded around with alarm in their faces but the priest stifled their questions with a stern shake of his head. At last the wild flow of words stopped and the boy slumped forward, resting his head on his arms. The priest looked significantly at Dolores and at his motion, she moved swiftly to the fire and brought a cup of steaming *atóle*. The priest lifted the boy's head and pressed the cup to his lips. The warm liquid brought a little color to the pale face and, when he finished, he spoke more calmly.

"Father, I come with bad news."

CHAPTER TWELVE

The little group was still, every ear listening, every eye on the boy. The priest fingered his crucifix. Antonio spoke, "This youth came riding hard. He was not looking for a trail, but he knew where to find it. How did he know?"

The boy swallowed with difficulty, "I am called Felipe, son of Augustino Sanchez, the *cábo* of our village, or what was our village," he covered his face with his hands and a shudder shook him. "Three days past, soldiers came to our *ranchito*. Ah, the horror. The blood and screams." He paused and the priest gently urged him on.

"*Sí*, Padre. I will try." He swallowed again. "They had heard, they told us, that a man had been to our village who had gold to trade for food. My father said this was true. That the man had come with a caravan from the north, going to Paso del Norte. He brought the little bag of gold to show. The Captain took it and poured some of the gold into his hand then he put it back and shoved the bag into his pocket. He said the man had lied. They had investigated and found no evidence of such a caravan on El Camino Reál, either to the north or to the south. Only in our village. Then the questioning began. They tied my father on a cross by the chapel." Tears started from his eyes and trickled down his cheeks. "We had finished it last week and the women had put flowers on the altar and hung a wreath on the cross. There he was forced to watch while they questioned our people. The Captain stood near him and watched too. The soldiers began with the women and children. They used branding irons and knives. Some of them restrained the men." He laughed, bitterly.

"My father was the *cábo*, the headman, and he felt their pain much more than if it was his own. At last he could stand it no longer and he shouted to them to leave the people alone. He said he would tell them what he knew." He stopped again. His face was contorted with the memory of the terrible things he had witnessed.

"And what did he know?" asked the priest.

The boy hung his head and sobbed. "It was my fault, Padre. I followed the man when he left our village and found no caravan. So I became curious. When I was hunting, one day, in the mountains, I saw your camp. Many times, I lay on the rocks above you and watched while you worked. This I told to my father, but he would do nothing. Not even when I told him you had a cave from which you brought rock that glittered in the sun. He said it was no business of ours and forbade me to speak of it." The boy broke down again in sobs.

"Ah, if I had only listened to him. He said no good, only

evil could come from gold, that wealth lay in the soil and growing things, which made everyone strong and happy. Perhaps the butchers of the King would have left us alone if it had not been for my curiosity. The guilt is mine that they are dead and our village burned."

"Go on, Felipe," the priest urged. "What happened?"

"The Captain shouted that those who lied and cheated the King must die and he ran my father through with his sword. I ran and hid but the screaming went on until at last there was quiet. Only the laughter and shouts of the soldiers. They searched but did not find me and when it was dark, I found a horse in the field and led him away very quietly. The next day and night I hid along the river. I thought to make my way north where no one would know me but I could not. I knew that my guilt would never leave me unless I came here to tell you. I could not let these cruel men find you without a warning."

All the emotion that had kept him going seemed to drain out of him with the telling and he sank down near the fire. A low moan went through the group, who had been listening, spellbound with horror.

"We must get away quickly," Elena cried. "Hurry! Take only what you can carry."

The women started scurrying about, picking up things and calling to each other to hurry. Antonio held up his hands and said, "Where can we go?"

Lucíta whirled to face him. "Where? Anywhere. Away, where the soldiers cannot find us."

Antonio went on, quietly. "Where can we go? If we go toward the mesas, that is the direction from which the soldiers will come. They will see us." He paused and saw that the women were stopping to listen. "If we go to the mountains, we will be hunted like coyotes through the canyons and peaks."

Ramon cried, "We can climb out of sight."

Antonio shook his head. "No. Perhaps you young ones, but not the older ones. The travel is too hard and slow. The soldiers would be after us before we could get far. And, if we lost our way, we could starve, wandering around for weeks. No fires, for they would tell the soldiers our locations and the high peaks already are dusted with snow."

The women were sitting despondently now. "Then what are we to do?" Rosa was crying.

Beltran answered her. "We stay and fight for what is ours."

"It would seem that we have no choice," the priest agreed. "We have toiled for this gold. The military have no right to come and take it from us. Let us take the gold bars from the *carrétas* and return it to the cavern with the rest. Perhaps, if they find no gold, they will leave us alone."

Antonio shook his head, doubtfully. "There is, perhaps, a slight chance. We can try and if it does not convince them, we can fight."

He turned to the men. "There is no time to sit here, wailing. You, *hómbres,* get the bars back into the cavern. It must be attended to quickly."

Estevan shrugged his powerful shoulders and led the way.

"Clear away," Antonio told the women. "Everything we have been using goes into the cavern. Let it look as if we were leaving emptyhanded." Turning to the boys, he called, "Ramon, Tirso! Get shovels and dig a pit. We must bury the debris from our work. Juanito and little Andres Cruz can destroy the water tank. Throw away the stones. There must be no trace of our operations."

"Estevan drive the stock up the slope toward the mountains. Get them out of the way. And when we need them we can bring them in. They will not go far from water."

Fear gave impetus to the work. Only the boy, Felipe, crouched, unheeding, in the bustle of activity around him. His eyes stared unseeing, the confusion of guilt and grief filled his mind. The priest looked at him, sympathetically, but there was no time to comfort him, now. A sick revulsion came over the father as he thought of the tale that the boy had told. The senseless brutality visited on the innocent people of the *ranchito*. The cruel, ruthlessness of the military was an old story. In his heart he knew that his people could expect no less. For himself, he did not care. Only the love and forgiveness of God was necessary.

Then the last of their belongings was carried into the cavern, Antonio looked about at the camp. Little remained of their life there. The debris of crushed rock, quartz fragments, and charcoal from the smelting had been raked into the pit dug by

Ramon and Tirso. Dirt was shoveled over, stamped down, and smoothed and the remainder scattered so that it would not attract notice.

"*Buéno,*" he approved. "Our enemies will see nothing to suspect. Now, let us look to our muskets. If we must fight, let us be ready."

Power and shot were divided among the men who had arms. Estevan grunted as he saw how little there was.

"*Pués,* Antonio. With this puny amount, we are to do battle with soldiers of the King? It is not enough."

"It is all there is, *mi amigo*. Except for a little to blow the entrance to the mine. Every shot must count. We can do no more."

"Then we had better be prepared to die," Fernandez retorted, walking stiffly away.

At that moment, a faint shout from the rim reached them. Pedro, who was watching the western mesas, beckoned and Antonio hastened up the trail. The priest stood, transfixed, with the others, their eyes on the two men as they conferred. Then Antonio started down. His first words confirmed their fear.

"It is the soldiers! We have, perhaps, two hours before they arrive. Juan Jose, you and Fernandez get your tools and begin drilling. Set the holes far enough back to collapse the entrance completely. *Ańdale, hómbres!* Lose no time."

He turned to the priest whose face was calm but very pale. "Padre, explain to the women what we have planned."

The priest, his eyes moving over the women, spoke hesitantly. "It has been decided that the only safety will be in the cavern and we ask you to conceal yourselves there and await the results of our encounter with the Captain and his men. We hope to convince them that we have searched for the gold and found nothing. That we are disappointed men, returning emptyhanded to the hacienda in Chihuahua. If they believe and go away, we will open the tunnel and all will be well."

The women looked at each other. Doubt crept into their faces as they thought about his last words.

"You mean, Padre that you will bring down the entrance after we are hidden?" Elena said. "This is not a good thought."

Seven Was the Padre's Number

Rosa's voice was harsh, "To be buried alive? *Que es ésto?* No! No!"

Horror and disbelief grew swiftly in their minds and the priest's answer was lost in the clamor of protest.

"This is not to be believed." Elena cried. "*Mádre mía!* To bury us like the rubbish."

"May the saints protect us," Luisa moaned. "That our Padre would consent to this. And you, Pedro, my husband, would do this terrible thing."

Antonio's bellow startled them to silence. "Quiet! You cackle like a flock of frightened hens. Understand that we are few against many. It will be difficult enough to face the soldiers, without women under our feet. It is the only way. Do you wish to be hunted through the sierras, cold and starving? In the cavern, you will have food, fire and water until we dig open the entrance."

"But you blast. The rock tumbles and fills the tunnel. Where are we then?" her voice shook.

"Aiee," the others wailed.

"A small amount only, Elena," Antonio soothed. "A little shot at the front. There will be some dust but it will quickly settle. It will take too long to cover the entrance with shovels. This way is quick and when the Captain rides out, we dig you out."

"You think they will listen and just ride away?" Lucíta said scornfully. "How much do they listen when they come to the hacienda? Or leave before they have what they come for?"

"We did not have muskets at the hacienda," Fernandez reminded her. "Now we are free men with the right to show force and we are armed."

"Then we will stand with you. We too have rights and will fight for them." Lucíta said stubbornly.

"*Sí!*" The women chimed in. "Not hiding in the dark, but here, in the sun with our men."

"What would you fight with?" It was Antonio's turn to be scornful. "Throw rocks at them? Scratch their eyes out? We do not have muskets to arm you."

Realizing the truth of his words, their valor ebbed.

"This plan is best for all," Antonio went on. "It frees the men of worry for your safety and leaves us to deal with our enemies."

"And if they will not listen and you are all killed? What then?" Elena was close to tears.

"You have shovels in the cavern. You can dig yourselves out," Antonio said firmly. "At least, the word will get back to the hacienda of what has happened here."

Grumbling, still uncertain, the women reluctantly moved to obey. The men looked to their arms and put a final edge to knives, already sharp. Antonio had his plan of defense. He stationed the men, scattered along the trail, behind boulders and brush, for cover. On the other side of the Basin, an arroyo cut down steeply into the bottom. It was deep and its rocky sides would afford protection as a last retreat. He pointed it out to the men. The priest refused to hide. He knelt by the ashes of the campfire, his lips moving in prayer. A shout from the tunnel and Juan Jose waved that all was ready for the shot. Antonio went to check.

"Where are the women? Are they clear of the tunnel?" he asked.

"*Sí*. I told them to lie down and hold their noses to protect their ears from the pressure of the blast." Juan Jose answered. "Shall I light the fuses?"

"*Un moménto*. The Cruz brothers are unarmed and can do no good with us. Also they are very young." He turned and called, "*Vénga aquí, mucháchos*."

When they came to him, he said, "Some of us should remain with the women. It will calm them and you can help to remove the fallen rock when we open the tunnel."

Obviously frightened, it took little persuasion to convince the boys.

Antonio spoke to Ramon. "Your mother would be much happier if you were with her. They need someone to take charge. Why do you not join them?"

Ramon hesitated. On one hand he would miss the excitement of battle. But, on the other, the thought of giving orders, particularly to Lucíta, was very attractive. And, if the battle were lost, it would be his job to lead the party back to Chihuahua.

"It is true, I have only my knife with which to fight. I will see that the women are taken care of," he nodded.

Waiting until his shout told them all was ready, Fernandez touched off the powder and the men ran to throw themselves on the ground, out of range. The explosion was followed by a gout of black smoke from the entrance and then a swell of dirt and rock heaved up, throwing debris high in the air. A long rumbling crash of falling rock came in a wave of muffled sound from the mountain.

Antonio raised his head as the dirt settled. Nothing remained of the entrance to the tunnel but a slight concave on the slope. The men got to their feet and he looked at Fernandez.

"That was a heavy blast, *hómbre*. You used more powder than necessary. From the sound, I fear the entire tunnel is blocked."

"Perhaps. At least our enemies will not find it. We can deal with the rock later."

"If we are lucky," Antonio retorted. "Well, what is done is done. Let us complete the work by rolling a few big rocks and some brush over it."

The priest turned pale as he grasped the meaning of what the men had said. "God forgive me. What am I responsible for? Grant me the hope that this will end right."

Dolores, unnoticed in the confusion of getting the women into the cavern, had slipped away. Even Lucíta's sharp eyes had missed seeing the girl vanish into the brush on the side of the peak. Her mind firmly made up to stay near the father, she had gone like a shadow without a sign or sound and did not stop until she was concealed in the deep arroyo that Antonio had pointed out to the men. The priest was mother, father, everything in her life. He had watched over the forlorn little waif, left alone in the world with the death of her parents. Her devotion to him surpassed any fear of consequences to herself. From her cover, she watched the blasting of the tunnel but she could not hear what was said. She saw the men scattered up the side of the Basin, along the trail, waiting for Pedro's signal from the top, and watched Juan Jose and Fernandez, their work done, move behind some boulders near the bottom. Twice she half arose to go to the Padre's side, seeing the distress in his face and knowing the agony of guilt that was wracking him. But, thinking of the anger that was sure to greet her, she sank back.

Bent to the work of concealment, none had noticed the cloud that had boiled high above the rim and across the sun, plunging the Basin into shade. Another followed and the air became sultry. The first boom of thunder warned them as big drops of rain began to splash about them.

"Get ready, *hómbres*. Cover yourselves," Pablo called and the men ran to find shelter under rocks and bushes.

The thunderstorms came up suddenly and fiercely, but did not last long. The rain lashed down and soon every depression was filled to overflowing. Water poured from the sloping sides of the Basin, cutting into the soil and loosening rocks that washed down with other debris in its path.

For half an hour, the men cowered, while the thunder growled and lightning crackled overhead. Then the downpour slackened and in a few minutes, ceased. Crawling out from under dripping bushes and glistening, rain-wet boulders, the men watched as the storm clouds moved west, over the mesas. The sun came out and the men stretched, gratefully, in its heat. The bushes and trees ceased dripping and the rain puddles disappeared into the earth.

"It is almost as if we had never been here," the priest marveled, looking about. "The rain has washed away all signs of our labor. Even our tracks are gone."

"*Mira*, where the trail descends from the *mina* the rain has washed the path into a small arroyo," Antonio laughed.

"It is most convincing."

At the first drops of rain, Dolores had found an overhanging rock and squeezed under it. After the storm, she emerged and looked back to see how the group blow had fared. They were standing in the sun, drying out. Voices and laughter came only faintly. Should she go down and join them. No, she decided. They would only be angry with her and she could not help. Better to climb farther up and keep out of the way. None noticed her as she moved furtively up the slopes, slipping through brush and behind jutting rocks.

Under the hot blue sky, the quiet of the Basin seemed oppressive. The priest clasped his crucifix to his lips and prayed that God would keep them all from harm. Antonio paced up and down, occasionally wiping the sweat from his face. The men squatted, talking among each other in low tones. Squinting at the sun, Antonio saw Pedro wave and start down.

"The soldiers of Spain are here," he called as he ran.

"They are starting up the canyon. Be on your guard, *amigos*."

"Get out of sight and wait," Antonio answered. Then he turned to the priest.

"Well, Padre, it will be soon now. Do you still think it best to talk to these men who come in the name of the king, their hands still bloody from putting the *paisános* of the *ranchito* to the question?"

The priest shook his head, tiredly. "No. It would do no good and, since our only advantage will be that of surprise, let us open the battle as they come over the rim."

"*Buéno*." Antonio called to the defenders. "Close up, *hómbres*. Take them as they come in sight, one at a time. Do not waste any powder. If one of you misses, the next man takes his shot. We will make them pay for the agony they cost the villagers who helped us."

The priest murmured, "God forgive me. I should never have let them come to this place."

Antonio grinned. "Do not blame yourself, Padre. Death is no different here than in bed at the hacienda. We have a fighting chance. Give us your blessing."

CHAPTER THIRTEEN

The air was sultry as they waited. The morning sun blazed down. The priest, raising his eyes to the hot, blue of the sky, noted a small gathering of clouds in the north. Perhaps another storm was brewing, not unusual at this time of year. Then he felt a little guilty. Having irrelevant thoughts of nature's moods had no place here, where a greater storm would soon break over the rim and spill down upon them.

Antonio felt the oppression in the air, as he went from one man to another, checking and explaining his plan of defense.

"Do not fire hastily, *amigos*. Let them come down to us. When I shout, pick them off and use care in aiming. Each shot must count. Keep down out of sight and change your positions often, if possible. Do not make it easy for them."

They did not have to wait long before the vanguard of the dragoons came, scrambling out the canyon and started down. As the soldiers looked into the great basin, they saw only the priest, standing below, his crucifix held high over his head. The sight of his robes and sacred cross gave them pause but only for a moment. Then others, crowding up behind, pushed them forward and with savage yells, they spurred ahead.

One of the colonists make an incautious movement that caught the eye of a soldier. At his shout, the concealing bush was riddled with shots from the trail. From the brush, Pedro rose to his feet, blood spreading over his shirt, then slowly bent forward to fall on the ground.

Even before Antonio's angry shout, the colonists retaliated and six of the soldiers fell, their frightened mounts rearing and pitching, throwing the line into confusion. Four more were knocked from their saddles before the men reined back to the rim. At Antonio's whistle, the men in the brush shifted their positions under the cover of the confusion, moving down a little.

The volley of shots brought the dragoons pouring up from the canyon, eager for action. The sight of the empty Basin with only the still figure of the priest waiting below, brought them to a puzzled halt. Questions broke.

"What have we here?"

"Where are the *paisános?*"

"What do you shoot?"

"*Que es ésto, Capitán Garciá?*"

The Captain, as puzzled as his men, reined to the side of

one of the wounded, a man whose shoulder was blown away. Looking into the tortured eyes he demanded, "What happened, Corporal Baca? Who shot you?"

The man rolled his eyes and waved a hand weakly. "*Capitán*, all I know, we saw the priest and started to ride down. Shots came from all around. *Cuidádo, Capitán*. These *paisános* are armed." His voice trailed away and his eyes closed.

Captain Garcia's face grew dark with anger. "Killing the King's men!" he cried harshly. "It will go hard with these *cabrónes* now! Spread out and hunt them down! A few roasted feet and they will talk. Then they can repent their sins before we kill them. After them!"

Forming a line, the horsemen urged their mounts down the slope. Antonio counted thirty-five men and the Captain, who remained at the rim, watching. He shook his head, doubtfully, calling to the priest, "Father, there are many and all with better guns and more powder. *Por favór*, get down behind this great rock. If you fall, the men will lose heart."

Reluctantly, realizing the truth of his words, the priest obeyed. He listened to the thunder of guns and horses above. Scattered fire came from the brush about them. The men were acting on Antonio's directions. Shoot and fall back, making every shot count. Occasional screams told that the soldier's fire had found a mark. However, the colonists were giving a good account of themselves. Used to depending on their skill for food, they now depended on it for their lives. As rider after rider went down, the charge faltered and turned back to regroup.

Antonio took advantage of the lull. "Into the ravine, *hómbres*. All of you. Be quick."

The men broke for the edge of the ravine that cut raggedly into the side of the Basin behind them. This was where they would make their last stand, win or fall.

The priest hesitated. "My people have died out there in the rocks and mesquite, Antonio. I want to go to them. They have given their lives and deserve to have God's forgiveness."

"No, Padre. Later that can be done. Now, the living need your encouragement." Antonio led him firmly toward the ravine.

Lucero helped the priest down over a rocky ledge. "Well,

Padre, we have reduced their numbers somewhat. God is with us." He winked cheerfully at Antonio.

Antonio counted the men. Eighteen, he made it and the two boys, Felipe and Tirso. He noticed that both had muskets and a pouch now. Tirso caught his eye and smiled, a brief grimace. He held up his musket.

"Felipe and I took them from the dead. They will not need them and we will see that the deaths are repaid."

Felipe nodded. "And for those who died in my village also," he said grimly.

"Si, hombres," Antonio agreed. "We lost good friends today and may lose more before it is over."

He turned away to attend to the business of war. Placing the men so as to cover the slope, they waited for the next charge.

"E-e-ho!" Estevan exulted. "We are doing well, *compádres*. There are not so many of the scum left, now. Excepting the brave captain, who remains safely above."

"I count twenty-seven," Antonio replied. "We have done it right. Remember, aim carefully and make every shot bring down an enemy."

The next charge was more cautious. The dragoons had more respect for their enemy now. These men, who hid like rabbits, had the eye and the strike of eagles. This time, they rode more discreetly, examining brush and boulders as they came, until a volley of fire revealed the colonists' position. Then it was too late. Leaving more men lying on the field, they broke back to the rim. The colonists watched as they huddled around the captain. Evidently a council for a new plan of attack. After a bit, eight men rode east along the rim. The force was being divided.

Antonio nodded his head. "Ah, they wish to get behind us. We will take care of that idea," he said, moving some of the men to the other side of the deep gully to watch their rear.

The remainder of the soldiers waited to give the detachment time to get into position. Quiet fell over the Basin. The wind was rising and the branches of mesquite and greasewood swayed with dry rustlings. Some of the soldiers dismounted to stretch and the men in the ravine relaxed also, still watching the soldiers. Then they saw them mounting, preparing for another charge. Slowly the descent began, the Captain remaining behind to observe.

The pace quickened and, as the horsemen drew nearer, spurs were put to the horses. Plunging down, their guns smoking, there was no response from the ravine. Waiting tensely, they heard the rattle of stones that warned of the men coming down behind. Then Antonio gave the signal and the guns began to thunder. Valiantly, they fought back but ammunition was running out. A final shot and they drew their knives, preparing for hand-to-hand combat as the soldiers dismounted and rushed them.

Furious at their losses and the frustration of being held back by this small band of sturdy peasants, the soldiers fell upon them savagely with their swords. Knives were no match for the long blades of Spanish steel or the thick leather of the dragoons' jackets, but the courage and desperation of the little group of men prolonged the inevitable.

Slowly the tide of battle turned against them as man after man fell. Beltran, run through, stumbled forward and thrust his knife into the throat of a dragoon and they went down together, their blood mingling as they died. Lucero, his head nearly severed by the swinging blow of a sword, great gouts of blood pumping from his body, crumpled at Antonio's feet. Retching at the sight, Antonio leaped at Lucero's assailant and slit his throat and then went down from a blow behind that opened his skull.

A blood-lust of killing drove the dragoons. Even after the last man of the colony was down, they stormed up and back in the ravine plunging their swords into the bodies and smashing skulls with their heavy boots. The Captain rode down to observe at closer hand. He saw the priest, his robe stained with blood, holding his crucifix on high, with a battle cry on his lips. Lunging his horse forward, between the priest and the fighting going on, he bent and threw an arm about the man. Then spurring his horse, he carried him a safe distance away and dropped him, unceremoniously, to the ground.

"Stay there, old troublemaker. I do not want you dead."

Returning to the battle scene, he shouted, "Hold! Hold! In the name of the King! Stop the killing. I want prisoners, not all dead men!"

It was useless. Wrapped in their bloody obsession, no one heard.

"Idiots! Imbeciles!" he screamed at them. "The dead cannot answer questions. I want prisoners, you fools. Someone who can be made to talk. To tell where the gold is to be found."

At last, their maniacal fury worn down, the dragoons clambered from the ravine and stood, drained and panting from the violence of their efforts. Only then did they become aware of the Captain. Containing his anger for the moment, he surveyed the quiet bodies before him in the ravine and then, his men, who looked up at him in bewilderment. They recognized his anger but, for the moment, did not understand it.

"Are any left alive?" he asked, chillingly.

The men looked at each other. "No one, *Capitán*," one answered.

The officer cursed them bitterly and the men shifted, uncomfortably, under the tirade of abuse. Then, his voice hoarse with anger, he said, more quietly, "Later, we will go into these matters more closely. Disobeying direct orders is serious. You were told to ride them down and take prisoners for questioning. Now we have only one prisoner and, but for my wit and rapid action, we would not have him."

The men looked from his pointing finger to the priest, who had risen and brushed the dust from his robe. He was standing, his face to the ravine, his crucifix in front of him and his lips moving in prayer for the dead.

"Gather the horses and tether them," the Captain ordered. "Then prepare food. After that we will put the holy man to the question. He undoubtedly knows all that we need."

"Grant me permission to go to my friends and give them last rites," the priest asked.

"Permission denied," the Captain replied harshly. "Renegades and traitors do not deserve consideration from the Church or the King."

"These men were not traitors," the priest said firmly.

"If we had found the mine of which we were told, the gold was to be taken to the Hacienda Aránda and the Church notified. Thus the church and the country would both have benefited, not these men, who only sacrificed themselves on a hard journey for the good of others."

"A most interesting story," the Captain said, his lips curling in unbelief. "And where is this gold, which was to be returned so unselfishly?"

"As you see, we have no gold. The man, who told us of the mine, was brought in from the desert, feverish and dying. It was foolish to have listened to him. We were preparing to return to the hacienda and tell them that the gold was only a dream in the fevered brain of a heat-crazed man."

"I also see no women," the Captain retorted. "We were told by the people of the Hacienda that your men took wives along."

The priest hesitated only briefly. Surely God would forgive a lie told to protect the women. "Some of the women became ill," he said. "They were sent back to a haciénda near Paso to wait for us."

The Captain considered. "I believe you lie," he said, his voice cold.

"Look for yourselves," the priest urged. "Do you see gold? Only the *carrétas* packed and waiting for departure. If we had gold, how could we carry it? In our pockets?"

"I think you lie, Padre," the Captain said. "I think you know where the gold is. We have ways of making liars tell the truth, as you will find out."

After the men had eaten and bound up their wounds, branches were lopped from the trunk of a cedar and the priest was bound securely to it. Captain Garcia watched with a cruel smile.

"Padre," he said, "You have given us a hard chase. The people of Hacienda Aránda were persuaded to talk freely about your mission. However, none knew where you were going. Only north. Beyond the Rio Bravo. Your passage was not too hard to trace. People remembered, with a little encouragement. The *paisános* of the *Ranchito* Sanchez on the river, were more stubborn. But as you see, we found you. And we do not intend to go back empty-handed. You will tell us the location of the gold or we will find ways to loosen your tongue."

The priest stood, his back to the tree, his eyes steady.

"My people spoke truly. We listened to the soldier before he died. We came, hoping to find the gold of which he spoke. He painted an exciting picture and aroused our enthusiasm but there was no gold. No mine. Nothing. We searched long and then decided that we had been fools. A little longer and you would have come upon us on the road back and would have seen there was nothing but supplies in the *carrétas*."

"Why then did your men open fire on us? Were their consciences so clear and blameless?" the Captain jeered.

"We saw you coming. I stood waiting to talk to you but your men shot down one of us on sight. Then we fought to defend ourselves," the priest said simply.

The Captain shot a glance at his men. Sergeant Martinez spoke hastily. "He lies, *Capitan*. Allow me to extract some truth from him."

"I turn him over to you, *Sargénto*," Garcia said. "His tone has the ring of truth but we can soon find out. However, let me caution you. Do not make a second mistake. You allowed your men to kill the renegades, although you were under orders to take prisoners. If the priest's words prove true, a number of citizens have been slaughtered which will look very badly in my report. A second mistake, such as letting the holy man die before he tells us the location of the gold, would have grave consequences for you."

Martinez' face paled. "The man lies. I am sure of it. But I will be skillful, *Capitán*. I will get the truth for you."

The Captain walked away some distance and stretched himself on the ground out of earshot and closed his eyes. The men sat down, their eyes fixed on Martinez and the priest, anticipating the cruel sport. Martinez took his knife from the scabbard and very deliberately prepared some sharp wooden splinters.

"Manuel," he said, "and you Esquibel, hold the hand of this *malconténto* who has turned against his Church and the King."

Seven Was the Padre's Number

The two men sprang, eagerly, to seize the hands of the priest, which had been left free when he was bound.

"Where is the *mina del óro?*" Martinez demanded.

"I have told you all that I can," the priest answered quietly.

Martinez pushed the splinter deep under the nail of the forefinger, as Manuel held it firmly out before him. The priest jerked at the pain.

"Where did the *soldádo* tell you to look?" Martinez asked.

The priest was silent.

"Light it," Martinez ordered Esquibel.

When it had burned to the finger, the priest screamed but did not speak.

"Where is the gold?" Martinez demanded and, when the priest still was silent, pushed another splinter under the nail of the next finger. Sweat poured from the priest's face and the smell of burned flesh floated in the air as they proceeded. After the fourth finger, he fainted. Water brought from the spring was thrown on him and he revived. The treatment continued on the other hand.

"E-e-ho," Esquibel marveled. "This man is stubborn."

Angrily, Martinez strode to his saddlebag and brought a chisel and hammer.

"Observe, *amigos*. This is my specialty. It will relax his stubborness."

He held the chisel to one of the priest's front teeth and tapped it, firmly. The tooth broke at the gumline and the priest fainted again. One after another the teeth were removed and still the priest would not talk. Pincers were brought and the nails pulled from his fingers but, although he screamed and lost consciousness with each one, he gave no answers to the monotonous questions about the gold.

Losing his temper, Martinez cursed as time passed. An ear was sliced away, then the other. Blood poured over the Father's clothing. He was only semi-conscious now. Although his eyes were open, he seemed neither to see nor hear. Excitement had risen among the watching men and they shouted jeering advice to the sergeant, on his lack of success. His anger flaring, Martinez cursed them and redoubled his efforts.

The Captain, awakened by the clamor, rose and approached just as Martinez, his temper raging out of control, plunged his knife into the priest's throat. Blood poured forth as the sergeant jerked it free and the priest collapsed in his bonds, looking like a bloody rag draped from the tree.

Wolfish howls broke from the watching men but silenced instantly at the Captain's shout. Martinez stood, his arms hanging at his side, transfixed by the realization of the enormity of his action.

The Captain's cold voice reached him. "You have finished, *Sargénto* Martinez? I assume, since the man is dead, that you have the answers to our questions." His voice was silky as he went on. "Can you tell me now the location of the gold?"

Martinez looked at him, helplessly. He knew, through the years that he had served under Captain Garcia, that there was neither mercy nor compassion in the man and he could only stammer, hopelessly, "No, *mi Capitán*."

The Captain's face hardened and his eyes bored into the frightened ones of the sergeant.

"What have you done?" he said, his anger rising, white hot, as the import of the sergeant's words hit him. "You have failed and the accursed priest has succeeded. Now it is too late. There is no one to give me the information I desire." His hand trembled on his sword and his face betrayed his urge to run the man through. Then his eyes went over the men and the sullen faces stopped him. They were close to mutiny. The circumstances were not good, alone here, far from any assistance. It was better not to push his authority too far.

He walked up and down, bringing his temper under control. Then he spoke in a more temperate tone. "What is done is done. Scatter out and search for the mine. Look for trails and for the dump, the waste from the mine."

The men hunted the slopes for an hour, while the sun declined. When they straggled back the Captain knew by their faces that nothing had been found. To his questions they could only shrug and spread their hands.

"There is nothing, *Capitán* Garcia," Martinez said. "The

paths are only here where they were camped and there is no sign of debris to be expected from a mine."

The Captain frowned. "Yet the man at the *ranchito* admitted they had gold. Why should he have lied?"

The men exchanged glances. "Perhaps, *Capitan,* he lied to escape further torture," Manuel suggested. "It has happened."

"The luck of the devil has followed the whole search mission. Since Father Sena sent for us, from the Hacienda Aránda at Chihuahua, we have had much trouble. It is what comes of getting mixed up in the devious turmoil of Church affairs."

The Captain strode about, glaring at the silent slopes of the Basin as if he could force them to give up their secret.

"You are certain, Martinez, that there are no trails into the hills?"

"No, *Capitán*. Only the paths about their camp which you see."

"They could not have worked a mine without leaving a trail in bringing out the ore. And they would have to dump the rocks of no use somewhere. I begin to believe that the holy man told the truth," the Captain said thoughtfully.

The men waited while the Captain decided his course of action. Then he spoke. "We will go back and report to Father Séna. If he desires another search, let him apply to the military authorities. Get your horses."

"*Sí*," Martinez said, his face brightening. "It is well to leave this place. I feel something evil in the accursed silence of this hollow in the hills."

Esquibel asked, hesitantly, "Should we not bury our comrades?"

"There are too many," the Captain said callously. "Their names will be in my report to our commander, as having died in his Majesty's service."

"What about the priest," said another. "Will it not be more bad luck if we leave him hanging there?"

The Captain hesitated. "Perhaps you are right. He was a renegade from the Church but he was a priest and he died bravely. Bury him."

A shallow grave was scooped out and the slight figure of Father La Rue was laid in and covered with earth. One of the men saw the crucifix where it had dropped from the priest's hand and took it, washing off the dark stains in the spring.

They mounted and rode up the trail to the rim. There Manuel and Esquibel paused to look back. Already dark-winged vultures were circling and Esquibel shuddered.

"That is how it is, *hómbres,* to die in the service of your King," he said to the others. "Look well, for someday it will be your turn."

Then they turned down the trail that led through the canyon to begin the return to Chihuahua.

CHAPTER FOURTEEN

Scrambling up the southern slope of the basin, bending low and twisting and turning to avoid the thorny branches of the mesquite that caught at her skirts, Dolores gained the top unnoticed by the men. On this side of the Basin, long ridges of weathered rock led back toward the mountains. Jutting, eroded crags, like breastworks, dropped away to the western mesas below. Cactus grew sparsely and here and there stunted pines struggled for existence with an occasional cedar.

A brisk wind whipped at her skirts and she shivered in her damp clothes. Over the rim a sun-warmed hollow offered protection and she went down to it, huddling under a twisted pine.

When the sounds of musket fire reached her, she sprang up and clambered back to the top. Cautiously, keeping out of sight, she peered around a great boulder and watched with growing terror, the progress of the fighting below. The agony and fear of the next hours held her in a paralysis of thought and action. Unable to move, she heard the roar of guns, saw men falling and dying, watched the annihilation of her comrades and later the questioning of the father, all as if it were a part of a terrible nightmare from which she would awake.

In this state of emotional shock, unable to bear the horror

of the scene below, she slid back down into the hollow, with no consciousness of having moved and crouched there through the dark hours, stunned. The night wind mourned around her in a lonely song of death. Thus she was unaware of the Padre's end or the dragoons' departure.

The dawn roused her and she tried to stand but cramped muscles would not support her and she sank back. Then the tears came and she sobbed disconsolately, as if she could never stop. The sun lifted over the mountains and bathed the land in golden light. Gradually her sobs ceased and she wiped her swollen eyes and stood up. The sun was warm on her shoulders and, unconsciously, she straightened them, preparing for the things she must do.

First, she must go down into the Basin and at the thought, dizziness overcame her and she trembled. Forcing herself, she half climbed, half crawled to the rim and looked down, a flutter of hope in her heart that some had survived. That she would see them gathered down there, the Padre and Antonio conferring, Tirso making a fire, and hear Juan Jose's hearty voice.

From the heights, the whole scene lay before her in deathly stillness. Quiet bodies scattered in the brush and along the trail, the ashes of the campfire and, to one side, the ravine where she could see more bodies, half hiden in the rocky cleft.

Slowly, she made her way down and walked to the edge of the ravine. At her approach, several vultures flapped away and perched on nearby boulders. The sight of what they left turned her stomach. Empty eye sockets and flesh stripped from the bone. She saw one of the heavy birds waddling back to feast and threw a rock at him. Then her stomach revolted and she vomited and sat down weak and faint.

A slight sound like a moan caught her attention and she stared into the arroyo, searching for a movement, any sign of life. She had almost decided that her ears were playing tricks, when she heard it again, close by. It seemed to come from under the stiffening bodies and bracing herself to touch them, she pulled at one. It came over and the girl looked into the staring dead eyes of Estevan. She clenched her teeth and pulled at the arm of another that lay across a third man. Pulling and tugging, she inched the body away and saw that the man underneath was Tirso.

His face, covered with blackening blood from a deep cut on the head, had the look of death but, as she screamed his name, his lips moved and he groaned again. Working frantically, she managed to free him from the weight of the corpse and saw that he was pinned down by a sword that had pierced his shoulder with such force that it was buried half its length in the ground.

Crying hysterically, she sought to pull it out but, not until she placed her foot on his shoulder and put all her strength into the effort, did it come free. A gush of blood followed the blade and she sat down in a wave of darkness. When it passed, she took off her slip and tearing a piece from it, went to the spring.

The dragoons had left a litter of pans, cups, and supplies scattered about the camp, after taking what they wanted and she found a water bag and filled it. Returning, she washed Tirso's wounds and bound them with strips from her skirt. All day she sat at his side, bathing his face with the cool water and anxiously watching over him.

Fever soon flushed his face and he muttered wildly in his stupor of the soldiers and the killing. Remembering how Elena had ground the roots of the moon lily and steeped them for a poultice when Lucero was injured, she searched for the vines, now dry and leafless. Gritting her teeth, she took flint and steel and a knife from the dead and built a fire. Cutting the roots to bits she made a brew and soaked pads to cover Tirso's wounds and bound them securely, for he was tossing and turning with the fever.

Finding a bag of ground corn, sacked for the journey home and overlooked by the soldiers, her spirits lifted and she quickly put it to boil for *atóle*. Holding the bowl to Tirso's lips she managed to get him to swallow small amounts. She dared not try to move him for fear of starting the bleeding, so she sat with him among the dead, threw stones at the vultures and prayed, fervently, that he would live.

On the second morning, she wakened to find his eyes open,

watching her with a puzzled expression. Tears sprang to her eyes and she bent over him to lay a hand on his forehead. The fever was gone and she began to laugh and cry, laughter and sobs mingling in hysteria.

"Oh, Tirso, I am so glad. It has been so terrible. All are dead and I thought you too might die and I would be alone here with no one."

Tirso's lips moved and he said, thickly, "What has happened? What am I doing here? Ah-h, the pain. My head. Call the Padre, Dolores. I must talk to him."

The girl quieted and her dark eyes filled with sorrow.

"The Padre is gone, Tirso. There is no one here but the dead."

The boy stared at her, his eyes dull, without expression. Dolores, the sorrow in her eyes changing to pity as she realized that he was still in a stupor, gave a long sigh.

"Tirso, I know this is very hard for you. Try to understand. It has been bad for me too. A nightmare of horror with no awakening because it is real."

Tirso put his hand to his aching head and felt the bandage. Vaguely thing were beginning to come back to him. The battle, the shooting. They had gone to the ravine, but then what? His memory would reach no farther. He stared at Dolores. Why was she here instead of in the cavern? What had she said? That all were dead? He tried to lift himself but a stab in his shoulder turned him faint. Dimly, he felt Dolores' hands pushing him down.

"No. No. Do not try to rise. You will start bleeding again," she said.

He heard her through a swirling darkness of pain. When he opened his eyes again, his head was clearer. He found the girl's hand and gripped it.

"Dolores, I must speak to the Father. Find him and bring him to me. Or Antonio. Anyone who can tell me what goes on here," he insisted.

"There is no one, Tirso. We are alone. Look about you at the dead. Can you not hear the *buáros,* the filthy birds that feed on our *compañéros*? I stone them but they will not leave."

Hesitantly, as if he feared to hear the answer, he asked, "All? All are dead? Even the Padre?"

"*Tódos muértos, aquí.* A-i-e-e." Dolores wailed. "It is a monstrous thing the soldiers have done. *Los póbres*. They fought bravely, so desperately, but those brutes, they swarmed over them, hacking and stabbing. I cannot remember. It was like a curtain drawn and everything was dark. Perhaps I fainted. I remember nothing until the sun came up and, at last, I made myself look again. The soldiers were gone, leaving this." She swung her arm about at the scene of desolation.

Tirso closed his eyes, trying to clear his mind that was whirling dizzily.

"The Padre is not among the dead," Dolores went on.

"It may be that the devil dragoons took him with them."

The two sat quietly, Tirso still overwhelmed with what he had heard. A thump aroused them as one of the vultures landed his heavy body and waddled forward. The girl seized a rock and screamed, "Get out! Get out, you filthy, black devil!" The stone struck the bird and it squawked and made an awkward, flapping retreat a little distance away.

"I cannot lie here." Tirso's voice was stronger. "Help me, Dolores. Get me up. Out of this place of blood and *calámidad*."

"What difference, Tirso. What can we do? Nothing. When help arrives, from those in the cavern, these *póbres* can be buried. There is nothing that we can do alone."

Tirso gritted his teeth. "Help me, girl," he said stubbornly.

Dolores shrugged and rose. Taking his good arm, she helped him gain his feet, where he stood a moment swaying dizzily and then sat down.

"You see?" she said, "you cannot stand, let alone climb out."

The determined gleam in his eyes answered her as he turned painfully over onto hands and knees and began to crawl upward toward the edge of the ravine. His progress was slow but, with Dolores helping, he gained the edge and rolled out on to the flat slope of the Basin. Here they rested. Tirso looked down into the crevice and spasms of nausea wrenched at him. His head throbbed and his vision blurred at the sight of men whom he had known all his life lying dead, cruelly butchered at the hands of the King's Dragoons.

As he stared, he saw with grim satisfaction, a few blue uniforms among them and said as much to Dolores.

"*Sí*," she answered, "and there are more along the trail, but not enough, Tirso. Not nearly enough."

After a little, she built a fire. "I will make some *atóle*," she said. "The soldiers ruined the camp but they left a little corn and a few things scattered on the ground."

Tirso watched her bending over the fire, the flames flickering on her slender figure and on her grave, sweet face. How fortunate, he thought, that she was here. He would have died in that foul ravine, except for her presence. When she brought the steaming bowl of gruel, he realized that he was famished and reached for it eagerly, gulping it down without waiting for it to cool.

"I did not know what great hunger I had," he said, smiling at her.

"You have not eaten for two days and you are weak," she replied.

The weakness will soon pass," he said confidently. He put his hand to his head and winced. "Ahé! *Tiéne múcho dolór*."

"*Póbre*," Dolores said, sympathetically. "A very bad cut, deep, to the bone. A little more and it would have split your skull in two pieces. It must have been your leather sombrero that saved you."

Tirso looked up, startled. "*Mi sombréro!*" he exclaimed. "Where is it? It was not destroyed?"

Dolores answered quickly. "Your hat was cut and full of blood when I pulled it from your head. I threw it aside."

"You threw it away," Tirso exclaimed! "It is a good hat. Don Tomás wore it with pride. When he gave it to me, I also wore it proudly. Bring it to me, girl. Let me see. Perhaps it can be cleaned and repaired."

Dolores made a face. "It is filthy, Tirso!" Then added hastily as he moved to get up, "But I will get it."

She left and Tirso watched her as she moved, hips swinging

slightly, towards the ravine, his eyes anxious. When she returned, she held the grey hat gingerly by two fingers, as far from herself as possible. He took it from her eagerly and his face fell as he saw the black clotted blood that stained it and a long slash near the top of the crown.

"*Póbre sombréro,*" turning it and examining the damage. "You have been treated badly." He thrust his fingers through the cut in the leather. "I let this happen to a fine thing."

"Not you, Tirso." Dolores clasped her hands. "You could not help what happened. The hat protected you. It may have saved your life."

"*Sí. Sin dúdo.* But it is destroyed. My fine hat."

Dolores' eyes were full of pity at his distress. "Let me try to clean it," she said, although the thought made her shudder. "Perhaps I can wash the blood from it and, later, you can mend it."

Tirso looked doubtful but he gave her the hat. "It can hardly be worse," he said.

"You speak the truth," she replied. Taking it to the little stream, she soused it vigorously and scrubbed the stains with sand. Then, pushing it into shape, she stuffed it with rags and, pulling the edges of the cut together, set it in a sunny place to dry. In the evening she brought it to Tirso and held it out for his inspection. He took it and turned it over and over, solemnly. Then he placed it on his head where it sat stiffly, high on top of the bandage. Dolores broke into laughter and, after a minute, he chuckled and then both were laughing for the first time in days.

"I will rub it until it is soft again," she said, "and it will be as good as new."

They slept soundly that night, huddled close together near the warmth of the fire. In the morning, the sun woke them. Dolores jumped up and stretched like a cat in the warm rays. Tirso sat up slowly, groaning at the stiffness in his shoulder and back. He watched as she built the fire and heated water to prepare food. As she bent, his eyes caught the glint as the little rosary that usually lay in the cup of her breasts swung free. She dropped it back into its nest as she straightened to bring him the hot corn gruel, her dark eyes smiling. His blood stirred and a message passed between them in his answering smile and in the touch of their hands as he took the bowl. Her eyes dropped behind the veil of her long lashes and she turned back to the fire for her bowl to hide the rising color in her face.

They sat, contentedly sipping the hot thick liquid, sharing the comfort of companionship. Dolores was mentally exhausted after the emotional shock of the past days and her eyes kept turning to Tirso, grateful that she was no longer alone, that there was someone who could make the plans and decisions for the days ahead.

The morning breeze brushed their faces, bringing the sickish sweet smell of rotting flesh. The girl set her bowl down, hastily, her stomach turning.

"Tirso, something must be done. The dead must be covered. We cannot leave them unburied longer."

"It is true," Tirso answered, grimacing. "But all those graves. Who can dig them? I have only one arm. I thought, by this time, Ramon and the others would have opened the tunnel and come to our aid."

"We cannot wait. Another day and the odor will be unbearable."

Tirso rose, holding his injured shoulder. "Can you find something to support my arm so it will not pull on my shoulder?" he asked. "That will free my right arm so that I can help."

The girl found a shirt in the debris of the camp and tore the back out to make a sling. As she tied it around his neck, Tirso's eyes looked deep into hers and her color rose again. She dropped her arms and started toward the ravine. Tirso followed, slowly. He was still very weak. On the edge they stopped and looked at the torn and mutilated bodies of men they had lived and laughed with.

"*Dios!*" Tirso said in a stifled voice. "What brave men are these, who fought to the end, against trained and well-armed soldiers."

"*Sí,*" Dolores replied, her eyes wet. "They fought like *tigres.*"

"You saw it all? The battle?"

"At first. Then it was slaughter. The soldiers were like savages, howling and yelling. Smashing and stabbing like fiends from hell. It was terrible. Their captain shouted to them to stop but they would not heed. Not until all, all were dead." A dry sob shook her.

Tirso put his arm about her. "I am sorry, Dolores. It was a terrible thing for you to see. It would have been better if you had gone into the cavern as you were told."

"I could not, Tirso. I wanted to be near the Padre. Would that *Diós* had let me help him. But there was nothing I could do. The captain pulled him from the fighting and, afterward, they tortured him. I could hear his screams but I knew that if the men saw me, they would use me to make him tell of the cavern and the gold. Then those in the cavern would have been at their mercy and no one left to tell of the evil deeds of those murderers. Now they will be punished. The Church and the King will be very angry with them, won't they?"

"I do not know," Tirso said sadly. "Perhaps." He shook his head. "Now we must do what we can for our *compañéros*. It is impossible to dig enough graves. Let the ravine be their *cámpo sánto*. Help me roll them into the bottom and push dirt and rocks down to cover them."

All day they labored at their grim task, until the bodies were well covered, beyond the reach of predators. Then, with dragging steps, pale and exhausted, they returned to camp, washed away the grime and tried to put away the thought of the crude burials.

In the night, Tirso heard the girl sobbing and pulled her close to him. Unable to sleep, he sought the answers to the questions that plagued his mind. Where was the Padre? Had the dragoons killed him? If they had forced him to talk, they would not have left the Basin. Then, where had they taken him? Another thing disturbed him. The women and boys in the cavern. Dolores had said that he had lain unconscious for two days and nights. It was two more days since he had opened his eyes and seen her bending over him. Surely enough time for the rocks and dirt to have been shoveled from the entrance. Were they waiting for the men outside to clear it? The women would be impatient, he felt sure, to find out what had happened in the Basin. Time would drag slowly, waiting in the darkness of the cavern and their anxiety would increase accordingly. There seemed to be no answers and he gave in to his weary body's plea for sleep.

The next day, the two searched the brush for those who had died on the slope in the early part of the battle. Where possible they rolled the stiffened bodies into depressions or crevices and scooped soil over them, piling stones on top. The dragoons Dolores refused to touch, calling them evil, vicious men who deserved no consideration.

Exhausted, with bruised and cut hands, they returned to camp, leaving graves behind them. Tirso halted as he noticed a mound of dirt and called to the girl.

"*Mira*. Here is one with no stones."

Dolores came closer. "It is not one of ours. See, there are marks of a shovel. The dragoons must have buried one of theirs here."

"Why would they bury one and not the others?" Tirso puzzled. He knelt down and dug into the side of the mound. A few inches and he pulled at a black cloth. Instinctively he knew what he had found and looked up at the girl, speechless.

"The Padre!" she exclaimed numbly and fell on her knees beside him. Clasping her hands, she rocked back and forth, crooning in a low wail of grief, tears pouring down her cheeks. Tirso pulled more dirt away, exposing one of the priest's hands. Dolores took it gently in hers and a low scream came from her throat as she saw the tortured, broken fingers. "The skulking sons of Satan." He got to his feet and shook his fist. "The torture and murder of this good and holy man shall be avenged. I, Tirso, pledge that. If it takes all my life, I will repay them."

Then he turned and began to gather stones, painfully, one at a time and toss them over to the girl. Tenderly, she pushed the dirt back over the blood-caked hand and joined Tirso, piling stones until a good-sized mound protected the body.

While the girl built the fire, Tirso forced his aching muscles to one more task. Climbing to the spot where the tunnel entrance had been, he lay down and pressed his ear to the ground. No sound of pick or shovel reached him, although he listened until Dolores called him for supper. A thought had been nagging him all day. Something Antonio had said after the explosion. Something about the blast having been too heavy and that the entire tunnel might be blocked. If that were true, it would take weeks for the three boys and the women to dig their way out.

When dusk fell, he broached the matter to Dolores. Silent and pale, she sat despondently looking into the fire. He put his arm around her and said, gently, "There is something we must talk about, Dolores."

She lifted her gaze to him and he saw her eyes were dull with grief.

"Tonight I listened for sounds of digging from the tunnel," he went on. "There was nothing. It is my fear that the blast was too heavy and brought down the rock from above, filling the tunnel. If this were not so, we could hear the sound of them working."

Still numb with pain and despair in the certainty of the priest's death, the girl listened almost without hearing.

Tirso spoke louder. "It will take them weeks and we can be of little help. Moreover, we have only food for a few more days. We cannot wait. I think we must go to the settlement on the river, called Socorro, and get men and tools."

"Help," Dolores said vaguely. "Yes, we need help."

"We have done what we can," he told her. "Now the best thing to do is to get men to return with us." He looked at her anxiously.

"You are right. Poor Elena and Rosa and Maria. All of the women will be frantic with worry. But who will tell them there is nothing left? Nothing but the gold." Her voice was bitter.

"Yes, it will not be pleasant. I would give all the cursed gold to be safely back in the Hacienda Aránda. The Padre tried to tell us that gold does not bring happiness but no one would listen. We have all paid a terrible price to learn the truth of his wisdom."

"In the morning we will go," he went on. "It is forty miles

to the river and then north to Socorro. We will need water and food." He took her hand and drew her gently down beside him. "Try to sleep. It will be a hard journey."

CHAPTER FIFTEEN

In the first gray light before dawn, Tirso awoke. He did not move but was instantly alert, waiting listening for whatever sound had roused him. Blinking his eyes to accustom them to the half-light, he made out a white shape by the stream. Instantly his mind told him what it was but he did not believe it. The rapid beat of his heart slowed and he reached out to Dolores' shoulder. His touch awakened her.

"*Mira! Mira,* Dolores," he said softly. "Like magic he appears to help us. Pardo has returned."

The girl rubbed the sleep from her eyes and peered through the dim light, following his pointing finger.

"*Grácias a Diós,*" she said, thankfully. "The good Lord saw our need and sent him to us." She broke into unsteady laughter.

The mule lifted his head from the water and blew his nostrils free. Then he turned his gray head to look at them. Tirso rose stiffly and went to put his arm around the old fellow's neck.

"Ah, Pardo, you are a welcome sight, old friend."

"I am glad to see him," Dolores said. "Now we will not have to carry the heavy load of water and meal across the mesas."

With the coming of the sun, they had eaten. Tirso braided a *ramál* from strips of the torn garments scattered about the camp. A shorter one was thrown over the back of the mule with a full waterskin and the bag of meal. Dolores had bundled up a pack containing two bowls and a pan, the flint and steel, and did not forget the tolache roots and some cloths washed clean for dressing Tirso's shoulder.

Standing on the rim, they took a last look at the Basin before starting down the canyon trail. A cold little shiver crept over the girl as they looked at the quiet sunlit slopes. She made the sign of the cross and murmured a few words of prayer. Tirso raised his good arm and made a vow to the silent dead. "We will not forget, *compádres*. We will return. And, somehow, I shall repay the unholy men, who did this to us."

At the foot of the canyon, they found the charred remnants of the two *carrétas* that had been loaded for the return journey to Chihuahua. The sacks of supplies had been ripped open and scattered over the burning carts. The waterskins were slashed. Only the great wheels were left, charred and split by the heat of the fire. Nothing was salvageable and they did not linger.

Pardo stepped out briskly into the deep grass of the mesa, setting a pace that was difficult for Tirso to keep up. By midmorning, he was staggering and even Dolores was tiring. They rested for a time and then took up the journey. At noon, Dolores insisted that Tirso ride for awhile. Long before dark, Tirso noted the girl's pallor and the dark circles of fatigue under her eyes and decided to make camp. He hobbled Pardo with the *ramál* and gave him a little of their water. Dolores made a small fire and cooked a little of the meal. Then she tended to his shoulder, putting fresh packs of the steeped roots on the angry, ill-smelling wound. The gash on his head was healing well but she shook her head and frowned over the other.

The second day they made better distance but Tirso's face was flushed and his eyes were bright with fever when they camped. He ate only a little and as soon as Dolores had dressed his shoulder, he fell into a restless sleep. The girl made up her mind that the next day he must ride.

Dolores woke with the sun to find the mule gone. Somehow, he had loosened the hobble and taken off during the night. Tirso was disturbed and a little angry when she wakened him with the bad news.

"*Cómo no*," he said in despair. "Did you not fasten him securely?"

"I did, Tirso. I tied the hobble just as you did. I do not know how, but the *ramál* must have come loose. I found it a little ways off, where he had stepped out of it." Her eyes were big and full of tears.

"Do not cry. It was my fault. I should have done it myself. Now it will be much harder to travel."

Seven Was the Padre's Number

The loose sand of the mesa made walking difficult and the load of the waterskin and meal was almost too much for Tirso in his weakened condition. They rested more and more often and, at noon Dolores insisted on taking a turn with the load. The weight of the bags cut into the tender flesh of her shoulder and she changed it from one to the other frequently.

By the fourth day they were both reeling with exhaustion. Tirso stumbled along in the heat, his eyes glazed with fever and pain throbbing in his shoulder. Dolores shook her head over it when she cleaned and dressed it that night. Although she said nothing, a fear was growing that they were never going to get through this barren desert to the river. The waterskin was almost empty and the two were nearing the end of their resources.

When she roused Tirso the next morning and got him to his feet, the thought of another day of broiling sun and sand was almost too much to face. The temptation to lie down and wait for whatever fate was in store for them, was strong. Then Tirso, his eyes fixed straight ahead, began his stumbling walk and the girl followed.

As the sun ascended, its rays beating down cruelly, their slow pace faltered and they fell often, each time finding it harder to rise. Her lips parched, she reached for the waterskin, only to find it gone. Somewhere, it must have slipped from her shoulder. Now, she thought, her head spinning dizzily, there was nothing but the river, flowing cool under the trees.

For some time she had been supporting Tirso, one arm around his waist and his arm across her shoulders. Her mind clung to the thought of the river, cool deep rushing water and she forced herself to take one step after another. She did not know when consciousness left her and she slipped to the ground and oblivion swirled over her. Tirso staggered on a few paces and then he too dropped to the sand. Neither heard the distant screeching of *carretas,* approaching from the south.

There were six large carts covered with canvas, supported on hoops. The advance riders spotted the two figures lying a short distance from the road. By the time the slow ox-drawn caravan reached the scene, the men had dismounted and found that the two were still alive although in bad shape.

Don Arturo de Aragon, who owned the caravan, ordered them placed on blankets in one of the carts and his wife, Dona Maria, who had some skill as a *curandéra,* supervised their care. She cried out in horror when she saw Tirso's condition and called her husband to see.

"*Los póbres!* What has happened. The young man has been run through with a long knife. It is bad. Already it smells of death."

Don Arturo shook his head. "I do not know. I have seen wounds like this on the battlefield when I rode with the dragoons in Mexico City."

His wife shuddered and protested, "Surely, even dragoons would not leave such young people on the road and a girl too."

Then she met her husband's eyes, her hand flew to cover her mouth.

"No, no, Arturo! The massacre of the people at the *Ranchito,* which we passed yesterday! Could these have been among them?"

"Be silent, my wife." Don Arturo frowned warningly. "I told you it is better to say nothing about what we found at the *Ranchito*. Remember, it is something about which we know nothing."

He rode away, shouting orders to the drivers and the caravan moved out. As they moved, the women applied wet cloths to the faces of the two and dribbled small amounts of water between their parched lips. Dolores was the first to open her eyes. Burning with fever, she muttered incoherently. Tirso like one in a trance, his face flushed, moaning in pain.

When the caravan pulled into the plaza of Socorro, Don Arturo sent a rider for the priest and turned the two over to him, ignoring his wife's protestations that she would care for them.

"No, my dear. I do not wish to bring these two strangers into my home. It is enough that we have brought them here. If questions are asked, I know nothing." He turned to the priest, explaining, "We found them by the highway, a day's travel south of here, more dead than alive from sun and thirst. The man has a nasty knife wound and a partly healed cut on his head."

They were taken to the one-room adobe home of old Juana, the *curandéra*. Juana had a vast knowledge of herbs and cures and she shut the door on curious eyes and tongues of the village, while she plied her skill. Under her care, they slowly improved.

Some weeks after their arrival in Socorro, the priest stopped to visit with Juana. After the usual talk about the affairs of the village, he brought the conversation around to the strangers.

"Where are your patients?" he asked. "I had hoped to talk to them about their plans."

"They are out under the trees, by the well. The girl is well enough and the boy is getting stronger."

"Have they talked to you? About where they came from and who they are? How did they come to the place where they were found?

Juana cackled. "They talked. Mother of God, how they have talked. At first, they did nothing but talk and plead for help. It made no sense. I think the sun addled their brains."

"What do you mean, they begged for help? Is it the same story those in the village are telling? A crazy dream of digging out a cave full of gold?"

"Part of their tale I can believe. That they come from a hacienda near Chihuahua. Her name is Dolores and she calls him Tirso. They have no family. This much seems true. But the rest, a-i-ee. What a story. Dead men and a priest killed by dragoons. Women buried in a cavern full of gold. They beg me to get men with shovels to dig these women out." She cackled again. "They promise wagonloads of gold. I tell you they were too long in the sun."

"So the villagers seem to think. It does sound a little wild. Perhaps you are right, it is only a sun-crazed dream," the priest considered. "After a time they will recover from the fever of the desert."

"Some do and some don't," Juana shrugged. "Now take old Teresa, who is no better than a child. You remember, Padre, when she was brought in. It was years ago that she was lost and given up for dead, until one day, the hunters found her. Better for her if she had died, wandering the streets and mewling like a cat."

"*Sí*, experience such as she had can be very bad," the priest agreed.

"Do you wish to talk to these two again today?" Juana asked.

"Not today. I have some things to see to at the Church. But soon I must have another talk with them. The story of a priest leading them disturbs me. I will pray that their minds clear and we can get at the truth."

Dolores and Tirso sat close in the shade of the great cottonwoods. They had been quiet for some time, their minds and hearts despondent at the helplessness of their position. The girl shook her head.

"What are we to do, Tirso? No one believes us. They think us mad."

Tirso struck his hand on the ground. "I have talked till I am hoarse but it does no good. Some look at me with pity, others laugh. It is no use."

"What is left for us, then?" she asked, her mouth drooping.

Tirso tightened his arm about her. "We can hope, *Chiquita*," he said grimly. "Hope that our people will escape by their own efforts. If that happens, the news will surely come along the highway. Then these stubborn fools will know that we speak truth."

Dolores nestled closer. "When people stare at me, I feel strange. Only when I am alone with you do I feel like myself. Do you think I am mad, Tirso?"

"No, of course not. If you are mad, then we are both mad with the same dream, as they accuse us."

They were quiet again for a time and then Tirso broached a matter that had been on his mind. "Dolores, since we are alone and wish to stay together, let us go to the priest, here, and ask him to marry us. Then no one can separate us."

The girl looked up at him with gladness in her eyes.

"I have wished to hear those words from you, Tirso, for a long time. Even before we left Don Aránda's hacienda. Our own good Padre knew my heart and hoped that you would return my love."

"I have been stupid. I dreamed of adventure and a bold life in the new country of the northern mountains. *Pués!* I have had adventure to last me the rest of my years. It is a bitter memory. Let us then go to the Padre soon."

"*Sí*," the girl said softly. "Perhaps the nightmare we have been living will pass with time and life will seem good once again."

Epilogue

Shadows lengthened and the room grew dim as the old man talked. Señora Aguirre lit a kerosene lamp and set it on the table, then retreated to the stove where kettles bubbled for supper. She smiled at the happy expression on the face of her husband. Seldom would anyone listen to his oft-told tale, but now, the men sat in rapt attention.

Mayor Rodriguez tipped back in his chair, his mind busy with thoughts of the possible notoriety that could ensue and might be used to his advantage in the coming election.

Father Markos was intent on comparing mentally the old man's story with the news reported in the paper. The archbishop in Santa Fe would be very pleased if a claim to such wealth could be proved.

The editor scribbled rapidly. What a story! In his mind it was already forming in black headlines and columns of type. The hacienda near Chihuahua. The dying soldier and his map. The brave little band led by Father La Rue, pushing north, stubbornly defying the hazards of the trail through the desert. The cavern discovered with its walls of golden wealth. The cruel massacre of the men and the cold-blooded killing of the father. The despair of the two survivors, unable to aid those in the cavern and their terrible journey across the desert for help, truly a journey of death. What a story! Edition after edition after edition floated before him. Papers would sell like hotcakes.

It was late and the stars were out when Senor Aguirre stopped. "That, *señóres*, is the story of my grandfather, the *Priméro* Tirso. Five generations of Aguirres and with each, the eldest son has been named Tirso. My grandfather and the girl, Dolores, were married in the church here in Socorro and lie now, together, in the *Cámpo Sánto* next to it. No one believed their story of the cavern of gold or those who were left behind in it to die."

The priest moved stiffly in his chair and said, "I can understand why. It is a tale that appears to be one of wildest imagination. But this discovery of the American's puts a new light on it. Did your report of the event not say that papers were found in the cavern? Perhaps among them will be proof."

"I got the story from Hot Springs and I have a copy of one of the papers. It seems to be a letter." Pembroke was searching his pockets. "Ah yes, here it is. It is quite long but the ending is interesting. It was written by Father La Rue and the date is 1802, to Father Rheuschone of Madrid, Spain.

> *In seven languages, seven signs and seven foreign nations, look for the seven cities of gold. Seventy miles north of Paso del Norte, in the seventh peak, Sóledad, a door deep in Cása del Cuéva de Óro, and receive health, wealth and honor.*

Father Markos struck the table with his hand. "There is the proof! Proof that the priest intended to inform the Church of the gold he had found."

Señór Aguirre rose stiffly. "You are right, Padre. And here is more proof." Going to the wall, he carefully lifted down an ancient leather sombrero and smoothed it lovingly with workworn fingers. "This belonged to my grandfather. He gave it to me before he died as a trust, because I alone believed him. It is the hat he wore when the dragoons struck him down. You can see, here, the hole torn by the musket ball that creased his skull. The sombrero saved his life. But for this, there would be no heirs to his treasure and no story to be told of the poor brave ones whose bones were found in the cavern.